Conger's Woman

Center Point
Large Print

**This Large Print Book carries the
Seal of Approval of N.A.V.H.**

Conger's Woman

RAY HOGAN

CENTER POINT LARGE PRINT
THORNDIKE, MAINE

This Center Point Large Print edition
is published in the year 2016 by arrangement with
Golden West Literary Agency.

First US edition: Doubleday
First UK edition: Chivers

The text of this Large Print edition is unabridged.
In other aspects, this book may vary
from the original edition.
Printed in the United States of America
on permanent paper.
Set in 16-point Times New Roman type.

ISBN: 978-1-68324-217-8 (hardcover)
ISBN: 978-1-68324-221-5 (paperback)

Library of Congress Cataloging-in-Publication Data

Names: Hogan, Ray, 1908–1998, author.
Title: Conger's woman / Ray Hogan.
Description: Center Point Large Print edition. | Thorndike, Maine :
Center Point Large Print, 2016.
Identifiers: LCCN 2016042527| ISBN 9781683242178 (hardcover : alk.
paper) | ISBN 9781683242215 (pbk. : alk. paper)
Subjects: LCSH: Large type books. | GSAFD: Western stories.
Classification: LCC PS3558.O3473 C6 2016 | DDC 813/.54—dc23
LC record available at https://lccn.loc.gov/2016042527

For those who complete the magic circle,
Lois, Gwynn and Mike—my family . . .

1

The saloon owner's name was Kennecott, Hunter recalled, digging deep into memory as he drew to a halt in front of the low-roofed, sprawling structure. Brushing his sweat-stained hat to the back of his head, he studied the bold printing on the sign affixed to its false front. KANSAS QUEEN, it proclaimed, and then, in smaller lettering below: GAMBLING-GIRLS-GOOD LIQUOR.

Hunter shrugged and swung wearily off his chestnut gelding. He wasn't interested in those tempting inveiglements at that particular moment; all he was concerned with was that Kennecott stake him to a square meal and help him get lined up for a job.

He grunted as his heels hit the ground, relief flowing through him at finally being off the saddle. It had been a long ride from Carson's Wells and the sun had been hot for September. He supposed his haste to reach Prairie City had been unnecessary, but the thought that Kennecott, with whom he'd become friendly some years back, could break the drought he was experiencing had pushed him hard.

Leaning against the chestnut, one hand gripping the horn, he glanced around, a slim, quiet-faced, light-eyed man in worn range clothing and run-down boots. Prairie City had changed little since he was last here, but it did seem busier. There were more people on the main street than he remembered, moving along the board sidewalks, some pausing to stare into the windows of the stores, others entering or coming out, while still more were gathered in small groups here and there. He frowned, trying to recall the date; it apparently was a holiday of some sort. A man drifting aimlessly about soon lost track of time, was aware only of seasons.

Hunter stepped up to the hitchrack, wrapped the gelding's leathers around the crossbar, mounted the wide porch and entered the saloon. It was dim inside, the wagon wheel chandeliers not yet having been lit, but there were several men gathered at the long counter, a dozen or so more scattered about in the area of tables and chairs reserved for gambling. Three or four gaudily dressed women were lolling around the piano near a small stage in a back corner of the room, all evidently awaiting nightfall, when business would pick up.

The interior of the Kansas Queen had changed, Hunter saw as he walked slowly toward the bar: new paint, more tables and chairs, larger mirrors, and he couldn't recall a stage for performers. But it could have been there; at the time of his last visit he was in more affluent circumstances and his interest and attention had centered on the games of chance.

8

"What'll it be?"

The balding, squat man behind the counter put the question to him almost before he reached the end of the bar.

Hunter nodded, said, "Kennecott. He around?"

The man shook his head. "Ain't here no more. Sold out."

Hunter swore raggedly. There was no breaking the bad run of luck that plagued him. It had begun over a year ago and dogged him with merciless persistence.

"Something I can maybe do for you? Name's Lat Miller. Was me he sold out to."

"I'm Jud Hunter. Looking for a job, figured he might know of something."

Miller drew back, folded his arms across his chest and considered Hunter critically. Jud could feel the saloonman's eyes raking him minutely, taking in his faded clothing, his neglected stubble, the unmistakable stamp of lean days on his features.

"Down on your luck, that it?"

Hunter grinned faintly. "Was I to say I've been eating regular I'd be lying."

"You particular what you do?"

"Not 'specially."

"Goddam swamper of mine showed up drunk this morning. Some chores around here need doing before the night starts. If you're interested—"

"I'm interested."

Miller bobbed, pursed his heavy lips. "Can't pay much. Your feed and three dollars a—"

"Suits me. It be all right if I stable my horse and eat first?"

The saloonkeeper nodded again. "Sure. Kennedy's barn's right around in back. Take your horse there, then get yourself a meal in the kitchen—right through that door at the end of the bar. You get your belly stoked, come back and I'll tell you what needs doing. What'd you call yourself?"

"Jud Hunter."

"Fair enough—but I'll kind of like it if you'll make it fast. Couple more hours and the crowd'll start pouring in. Want to be all set."

"Sure," Hunter said and, wheeling, returned to the street.

He swung onto the saddle and rode the chestnut down the side of the Kansas Queen to the livery barn Miller had indicated. An overalled hostler, tobacco juice staining his beard, moved indolently from a small office in the front of the structure to meet him at the entrance. Jud pulled to a stop, again dismounted.

"Working for Lat Miller," he said. "Told me to stable my horse here."

"Figures," the hostler said.

Hunter frowned. "Why?"

"Owns the place. Owns about half of everything else around here, too. How long'll you be staying?"

"Can't say. Just filling in for somebody that showed up drunk."

"Old Anse," the hostler said, and jerked a thumb at a man sleeping on a cot in the office. "Got so's he's falling down drunk most of the time nowadays. Expect you can have his job permanent like was you to ask Lat for it."

"Swamping's not exactly the kind of work I'm used to doing."

The hostler's shaggy brows lifted. "No? Well now, just what kind of work are you used to doing—banking, maybe?" he asked slyly, taking in Hunter's bankrupt appearance in a sweeping glance.

"Nope," Jud replied coolly, "but it ain't swamping in a saloon. . . . Horse could use a rubbing off and I'd consider it a favor if you'd grain him some."

The old man shrugged. "Sure. Whatever you want. You leaving that rifle?"

Hunter's eyes went to the weapon riding in its scarred saddle boot. Outside of the horse, his bridle and hull and the belted gun around his waist, it was the last of his gear yet unsold. Chaps, silver belt buckle, extra spurs—all had been cashed for grub months ago.

"Aim to unless you figure it's liable to get stole."

"Can't give you no for-sures."

"I see. Well, I'm not sure where I'll be sleeping

tonight. Soon's I find out, I'll come back for it."

The hostler's shoulders twitched again. "Up to you." He pointed to an empty stall halfway down the row. "Horse'll be in there. Tack'll be straddling the wall alongside. Don't go waking me up if I'm sleeping."

Hunter grinned, said, "Obliged," pivoted and walked back to the saloon.

He located the back door, entered and found himself in a narrow hallway. At its far end he saw the door pointed out earlier by Lat Miller and, judging from its location and the smell of food cooking nearby, guessed the kitchen lay behind one of the scarred panels that opened off to his right.

Reaching the first, he twisted the knob and entered. He had guessed right. In the back corner of the room was a large square-topped cookstove. Cabinets and well-stocked shelves lined the adjacent walls, and in the center of the area there were several tables and chairs. A large raw-boned woman with a heat-flushed face and stringy gray hair looked up at his entrance.

"Reckon you'd be Hunter," she said, laying down the knife with which she was slicing potatoes. She wiped her hands on the apron she wore. "I'm Mattie Fergusson. Folks call me Ma. Set down and I'll feed you."

Jud crossed to one of the tables, settled onto a chair. The woman brought a cup of steaming black coffee, placed it before him and returned to the stove.

"Come for the hanging?"

Hunter swallowed a mouthful of the liquid, eased back gratefully. It was like pouring new life into his jaded body.

"Nope, come looking for Mark Kennecott. Was hoping he could line me up with a job." He paused, frowned. "That what's making the town look busy—a hanging?"

"Drawing folks like honey draws flies."

"Usually does. Who's getting hung?"

"Auralee Ford."

Hunter set his empty cup on the table as surprise jolted him. "A woman?"

Ma Fergusson came forward, a plate of fried meat, potatoes and thick gravy in one hand, a basket of biscuits in the other, all evidently prepared beforehand in readiness for the evening rush.

"A woman," she said. "First one that's ever got herself hung in these parts."

"First one I reckon I've heard of getting hung anywheres," Hunter said, picking up his knife and fork and beginning to eat. "When's it going to happen?"

"Noon, day after tomorrow. They sure are making a show of it," Ma added. "Can leave it up to the merchants to cash in on it. Folks coming in for a hundred miles around."

Jud munched contentedly at his food, enjoying

each bite. It was his first complete meal in months and a far cry from the hard, grease-soaked fried bread and occasional rabbit on which he'd been subsisting.

"What did this Auralee do?"

"Murdered her husband—Emory Ford. Big rancher west of town. Rich, him and his brother, Tom. Plenty big shucks in this country, get anything they want."

Jud paused, considered the woman now leaning against the wall, arms folded across her ample bosom. He thought he detected a note of derision in her tone.

"There some doubt she didn't do it?"

"Claims she didn't. Jury and the judge figured different."

"That maybe because the Fords are such big shucks, like you said?"

"No, ain't saying that's got anything to do with it. Reckon she's guilty, all right. Was only meaning that Tom Ford could have made it turn out that way whether she was guilty or not, was he of a mind."

Hunter shoved his empty cup across the table. Ma procured the large granite pot from the stove and refilled his container.

"I savvy," he said. "Seen a few like him before. Get what they want no matter what."

Ma nodded, eyed him thoughtfully. "Aiming to hang around?"

"Depends on finding myself a job. What I come here for—work."

"Lat'll probably keep you on swamping—"

"Not what I'm hunting. Punching cows, or maybe driving for some freight outfit or stage line—that's what I do best."

"Well, you picked a good time to come looking. Expect every rancher in this half of the state'll be here, not to mention all them others that's coming to see the fun. . . . You want another piece of meat?"

"Sure would appreciate it. Don't mind saying this is the best meal I've had in years."

"Glad to hear it. Most folks eat just to be eating and because it's something they have to do. How about some more spuds?"

"Steak'll do me fine. Besides, I got to be getting in there and earning my keep."

Ma Fergusson laid a hand-sized slab of meat on Jud's plate, refilled his coffee cup once more. "You finish with that I'll bring you a dish of fresh apple flummery. Beats pie any day of the week. . . . You was speaking of Kennecott. You a friend of his?"

"Got sort of acquainted when I was here a few years back."

"Was a fine man. Took me in and give me this here job when my mister got hisself killed—"

"Was?" Hunter repeated, pausing.

"Dead now. Shot while he was crossing the street. Nobody ever found out who done it."

Jud considered that for a time as he chewed on a piece of the meat. Then, "Was that before or after Miller took over this place?"

The woman shook her head. "Now, don't go making something out of that. Was a long time after. Was no doings of Lat."

"Just wondering," Hunter said. "Town sure has changed. Was real peaceful before. Now it's got plenty wild—somebody killing a man like Kennecott, a woman killing her husband and about to get hung. Sounds more like Dodge."

"You'll think it's Dodge once they come piling into the saloon tonight," Ma Fergusson said, turning away. "Seems more like a circus going on than a hanging, but I reckon folks ain't never seen a woman swinging from a gallows tree—'specially one like Auralee Ford."

2

Only the men playing cards at the tables were still in the saloon when Jud Hunter returned to assume his duties. Miller, lounging against the bar, moved out to meet him as he came through the doorway.

"Took you long enough," he grumbled, and pointed to a bucket of water and a heavy corn broom. "First thing off, you'd better sweep. Wet the broom so's you won't raise no dust."

Jud nodded and fell to the chore, starting at the rear of the wide room and working toward the front. He performed the task mechanically, giving it little thought, his mind elsewhere—on the long miles behind him, on the hanging of Auralee Ford, on the good opportunity for finding a decent, suitable job with one of the ranchers in town for the event. Surely there would be one cattle grower among them who would be in need of an experienced hand.

He finished the sweeping with only a small amount of muttering from the men at the poker tables and reported to Lat Miller for further instructions.

"Going to need more light," the saloonman said, glancing up to the big wagon wheel chandeliers suspended by pulley and rope from the ceiling.

17

"Been using only about half of what I got—figure it's best now I use them all. Means filling the lamps and trimming the wicks. You'll find a barrel of oil and a can in the back room."

Hunter made no reply, simply sought out the kerosene, unloosened the first rope secured to the wall by a hook, released it and lowered the painted, spoked fixture. There were six lamps and he dutifully filled and pared the wick of each, wiping the accumulated smoke and dust film from the glass chimney as he did.

"Might as well light them now," Miller called from his place behind the bar. "Save doing it later."

Jud complied and, the first of the fixtures completed and aglow, he drew it back to its overhead position, fastened the rope into place and passed on to the next. It was good to be working, to be doing something—even the menial tasks of a saloon swamper.

By the time he had finished the last of the four chandeliers darkness had closed in and the patronage of the Kansas Queen had increased. Half a dozen men were now at the counter being served by Miller's regular bartender, now on duty. An elderly woman pianist, hired probably for only the duration of the anticipated festivities, was at the music box, where she was picking experimentally at the keys.

More girls were in evidence, several wandering

listlessly about among the tables where the card players had more than doubled in number. Hunter, halting just outside the door after returning the oil to the storage room, felt a twinge as he watched the men at their game, listened to their terse comments, heard the sharp click of coins and dry snap of the cards.

Not too many years ago he'd sat in that very room, at those same tables and played out the hands dealt him. Like as not he'd opposed some of those very men now enjoying the game. He'd done right well in the Kansas Queen and then he'd moved on to the next town—hell, he wasn't even sure of its name now—and lost his stake. That's the way it went: win in one place, lose in the next. If a man could ever get a win streak going and keep it going he could—

"Hunter."

At Lat Miller's call Jud crossed to the end of the bar.

The saloonman said: "Reckon you can do some table waiting?"

Hunter shrugged. "Never tried it, but I never tried swamping before either."

"It don't call for much. Carrying a bottle and some glasses and then collecting for it. Sometimes it'll maybe be a tray and a round of drinks."

"Willing to try if you say so."

The piano player struck up a tune at that moment and a burst of cheers echoed through the saloon. Smoke was beginning to hang in restless layers close to the ceiling and the steady undertone of voices was growing.

"All right, just hang around here close to the bar. We'll holler when we need you."

Incoming traffic had increased to a continuous flow and the saloon was filling rapidly. Two of the girls had mounted to the stage and were rendering a ballad to the uncertain accompaniment of the piano. The song was not half bad, but their efforts received scant attention and when they had finished there was only a smattering of applause.

"Back table—over there," Miller said, sliding a tray with a bottle and half a dozen glasses toward him. "Collect two dollars."

Jud took up the wooden plate and, steadying the bottle with one hand, made his way through the crowd to the players indicated. Setting the glasses and the liquor before them, he said, "Two dollars."

One of the men flipped the coins onto the tray, grinned. "Can't say as you're the prettiest waitress I've ever seen—"

"Ain't supposed to be," Hunter replied, and wheeled about. He checked abruptly, colliding solidly with someone crossing behind him.

"Dammit—watch where you're going!" the man shouted, and lashed out with his opened hand.

The blow caught Jud across the face, sent a wave of anger racing through him. He spun, dropping the tray he was holding onto the table beside him, and drove his fist into the belly of the redheaded man glaring at him.

The man gasped, swore deeply, struck out again. Hunter blocked the swing with his left forearm, sent another knuckled fist into the redhead's middle, followed quickly with a left jab to the nose. Around him the saloon was in sudden turmoil. Men were yelling encouragement, giving advice. One of the girls had climbed onto a chair and, eyes bright with excitement, was screaming something at him. Somewhere amid the confusion Hunter thought he could hear Lat Miller's voice, but he gave it no thought.

He drew back, seeing the squat redhead moving toward him fast. Stepping to one side, he came up against a chair, began to fall, caught himself. Half down, he jabbed again with his left, stalled the man, and then again his feet squarely under him, nailed the redhead with a hard right to the jaw.

The husky man staggered, fell across a table. Only then did Hunter see the star with the words DEPUTY SHERIFF engraved blackly upon it. He straightened, a wry, frustrated sort of anger gripping him. *A lawman! Why the hell did it have to be a lawman?*

The shouting began to die as the lawman, gun now in hand, drew himself erect slowly. His eyes were snapping and there was a hard set to his mouth.

"All right, you goddam saddlebum, I'm taking you off to the jug."

Hunter stiffened as a chorus of protests sounded. A man directly behind him pushed forward.

"Aw, what's eating you, Keeter? Was you that started it."

"Makes no nevermind. Ain't nobody going to roust the law around this town."

"He sure'n hell done that!" a voice back in the crowd yelled.

Keeter's face darkened as laughter broke out. He glanced at Jud. "Come on—get your stuff."

Lat Miller shouldered his way into the circle, took a stand beside Hunter. "Now, hold on a minute, Ed. You got no call arresting him. Was your fault, not his. Seen you bump into him myself."

The deputy shook his head. "Had no business using them fists of his'n—"

"Was you that started that too."

Keeter said, "The hell. Was him that hit me first."

Miller waited until the denials of bystanders had died, faced Hunter. "That so?"

Jud reached out his hand, passed over the two silver dollars clenched in his fist. "No, was him."

"Only give you a push—getting you off my foot," Keeter said stubbornly. "Don't make no difference, nohow. I'm locking you up. Get your gear if you got any."

Jud shrugged, moved off through the crowd toward the bar, where he'd stashed his hat, jacket and gun belt. Ed Keeter followed closely.

"Don't do no fretting about it," Miller said, stepping up beside him. "I'll go get Rufe Gosset—he's the sheriff—and tell him what happened. You'll be out of there in thirty minutes."

Hunter nodded. He picked up his gear, passed the gun to the deputy, pulled on his hat and, slinging his worn jacket over a shoulder, crossed to the saloon's entrance and stepped out into the street.

The walks were still crowded, but few noticed him and the blocky shape of the deputy as they cut right and marched the hundred yards or so to the square rock structure that served as Prairie City's jail.

They entered the dimly lit office and Jud paused while the lawman, grimly silent, unlocked a drawer in the desk and procured a ring of keys.

"Through there—and don't try nothing cute," Keeter ordered, pointing to a door in the back wall.

Hunter moved ahead, drew open the heavy panel and walked into the room in which the cells were built. The bracketed wall lamp had been turned down, but he saw immediately that there were two cages and that one was occupied. The prisoner rose slowly as they crossed to the door of the cell adjoining—a slender, well-developed, startlingly beautiful woman clad in a light-colored dress.

Hunter stared at her transfixed as he waited for Keeter to unlock the grill. She returned his study with a quiet gravity, her large almond-shaped eyes—blue, he thought, but they could be gray—meeting his frankly. This was Auralee Ford, he realized, and understood then what Ma Fergusson had said about her and the people who had come to watch her die.

"She's a real looker, ain't she?" the deputy said, opening the cell. "Well, don't let that fool you none. That there gal's one third timber wolf and two thirds rattlesnake and for a heart she's got a lump of solid granite."

Jud walked into the cage silently and halted, flinching as the door clanged shut and the lock flipped into place.

"Ought to be some place better'n in here to keep her," he said finally as the deputy moved away.

Ed Keeter paused. His puffed lips pulled into a scornful grin. "Well, now, you ain't got nothing to be scared of, cowboy. She can't get to you through them bars."

"Wasn't thinking of that. Just no place for a lady—"

"She's right where she belongs," the deputy said, "and right where she's staying until we get ready to stretch that there pretty neck of hers. . . . You just pile yourself onto that cot and, come morning, I'll see about turning you loose."

3

In the hush that followed the deputy's departure Hunter could hear the quiet sound of Auralee Ford's breathing.

"Do you believe what he said about me?"

At her question he turned slowly. She was facing him, her features soft and shadowy in the yellow lamplight.

"Don't know anything about it," he said after a time, but he was finding it hard to believe this striking, almost delicate girl-woman could be a killer.

"But you do know I'm to—to hang?"

She had a low, somewhat husky voice that suggested education and a genteel background.

"Was told that."

"I didn't do it!" she said in a sudden burst of desperate words. "You must believe me—I didn't murder my husband!"

Abruptly she sank onto her cot and, lowering her head, began to weep softly. "I didn't—I didn't," she murmured.

Jud moved up to the wall of bars that separated them. He listened to her muffled sobbing for a long minute and then sighed.

"Was a jury—and a judge," he said heavily. "They must've figured you were guilty."

Auralee looked up. "They did what Tom Ford wanted them to do. He hated me from the start."

There could be something to that, Hunter thought, recalling other things Ma Fergusson had said—that the Fords wielded powerful influence in that part of the country, for one.

But his question was blunt, indifferent. "Why?"

Auralee opened the small flowered reticule that dangled from her wrist and drew out a lace-edged handkerchief. Dabbing at her eyes, she again rose to her feet, and smiled at him through the bars.

"I'm sorry about breaking down," she said. "I—I just couldn't help it. Everyone is against me—are so set on punishing me for something I didn't do. And I can prove I'm innocent if only they'd let me."

The light, sweet odor of lilac filled Hunter's nostrils. Perfume on her handkerchief, he supposed. Jud savored it for a bit, shrugged.

"You tell them that?"

"Of course I did, but they wouldn't listen. Tom Ford's the only one they'll pay any attention to. Everybody around here is afraid to go against him."

"If you didn't kill your husband, who did?"

She gave him a quick, angry look. "You see? You think I'm guilty, too, without even—"

"Never said that," Hunter cut in. "But the law must've figured that's the way it was or you wouldn't be in here."

26

"I wouldn't be in here if it wasn't for Tom Ford," she retorted. "You asked me who shot Emory—I don't know. Someone hiding in the bushes. Could have been Tom, for all I know."

"His own brother?"

"Yes, his own brother. There was bad feeling between them—always was, I guess. It became worse after Emory and I were married."

Hunter considered that in silence. Somewhere down the street a gunshot cut through the night, disturbing a dog that began to bark in a steady, monotonous way.

"You live here then?"

"No, New Orleans. That was my home. Emory came down there on a trip of some sort. We met and were married a few days later. Tom was really angry when we got back and he learned of it."

"Some reason for that? Emory too young maybe?"

"No, he was almost thirty, so that wasn't it. I think he just hated Emory and when he returned with me it grew stronger. He was always picking at him, trying to order him around, make him do things. They were equal partners in the ranch— their folks left it to them with that under- standing—but Tom wanted to be the big boss and run things his way."

"How'd Emory take it?"

"Never let it bother him much. He was a happy-go-lucky man, never worried about anything. I—I loved him."

Hunter was again quiet. Men were shouting in the street now, their voices barely audible inside the thick stone walls of the jail. The barking dog had acquired several echoes.

He heard her move away from the intervening bars and raised his glance to follow. She halted in the center of her cramped quarters, once more touching her eyes with the bit of lace and linen. The dress she wore was of some soft knitted material, fit her body closely, outlining her figure to perfection. A thought came to him.

"Could be this Tom was jealous of his brother—him bringing home a wife like you."

Auralee wheeled slowly, a frown on her pale, lovely face. "I never thought of that," she said. "It could be. He's the older of the two. Maybe he felt he should be the one to marry first and when Emory found a wife before he did—"

And one like you, at that, Hunter added mentally, but he said aloud: "Happens that way sometimes."

But it could account for the increased bitterness Auralee said existed between the two brothers, and when Emory had been bushwhacked, Tom could have taken advantage of the situation to vent his vindictiveness on her. . . . The corners of Jud Hunter's mouth pulled suddenly into a hard grin; he was going right along with Auralee Ford, accepting her claim to innocence, ignoring the findings of a judge and jury on something he knew very little, if anything, about. Still, the law had made mistakes in the past, it could be making one again.

"You said something about proving you didn't shoot your husband."

"I can!" she replied hastily, and returned to the grillwork that stood between them. "I have a friend—some friends who will help me if I could just get out of here."

"Not much time left. Two days, less."

She bit at her lower lip. "It would take longer than that; but what difference would it make? The only ones who'll be disappointed in not seeing me hang are Tom Ford and his crowd. And if I proved I wasn't guilty the law would be satisfied."

"Reckon so, but I don't see much chance of you breaking out of here."

"I suppose not," she said drearily. "I'm—I'm just helpless. I can't do a thing to help myself. Everybody refuses to listen to my side of it."

"You tell that to the jury?"

"I tried, but they had their minds made up even before they heard what I had to say. And then they just ignored me."

There was less noise in the street now. Apparently the matter of the gunshot had been cleared up, whatever its cause, and things were restored to normal. All the saloons would be doing a brisk business while the families of the outlying ranchers, there for the occasion, would be visiting in the homes of friends. Even the dogs had fallen silent. . . . He should be getting let out of his cell, it seemed, if Lat Miller was going to come through as promised.

He slid a covert glance at her. There was a haunting quality to her beauty, an essence that touched him deeply.

"Sure wish there was something I could do for you," he said lamely. "Maybe was I to talk to the sheriff, get him to hold off for a few days while I see these friends you were talking about."

"He wouldn't do that. Tom would never stand for it. The only answer is for me to escape."

Hunter shrugged, looked about at the solid walls. "Not that kind of a jail."

"I realize that, but it's the only way. Maybe once they let you go you could find a way."

"Don't hardly see how."

"I can't either, but it's the only answer. And forget that I asked you to help. It would mean trouble for you."

"Me and trouble are old friends. I'm kind of used to it. Wouldn't matter anyhow if you proved them wrong. They'd forgive me right along with begging your pardon."

She leaned toward him, features tense, her eyes mirroring the hope stirring within her. "Do you mean that maybe you can think of a way to help me, Mr.—I don't even know your name."

"Jud. Jud Hunter, without the Mister."

"I'm Auralee Ford—but you know that," she said with a short laugh. "Oh, if you could only help me get out of here long enough—"

"Might work out something—not sure what."

"We would have to get the key. They're kept in a drawer in the sheriff's desk."

"I know. Could pry it open easy enough. It's the getting back inside here once they let me out and doing it without being seen that'll be the puzzle."

"You could early in the morning. There won't be anybody on the street and the deputy will be in there sleeping."

"He spend the nights here?"

Auralee nodded. "I can hear him snoring some-times. You'd have to knock him out."

Hunter rubbed thoughtfully at the back of his neck. He was slipping into a plan designed to help Auralee Ford escape and was hardly conscious of it, but somehow it seemed right. If she wasn't guilty of her husband's death, and because of Tom Ford's influence wasn't being allowed to prove it, she should be helped.

"Could be trouble there too. Likely keeps that front door locked once he closes up for the night."

She frowned and bit at her lip again, a childlike, petulant trait. "I never thought of that—but there should be a way around it, Jud. There just has to be!"

"Was a window, I recollect. Not sure if it had bars. If it doesn't I might be able to leave it unlocked while I'm standing there waiting for the deputy to get my gun out of the desk drawer where he put it."

"I'm not sure either about the bars although I've been in there several times. Couldn't you fix the door?"

"It's probably got a bar that he drops into place, besides having a regular lock. If that's the how of it then we can forget it. Never noticed if there was a back way into the place."

"There is," Auralee said promptly. "Door at the end of that hall that runs past the cells. The sheriff's wife comes for me every day, takes me to their home so's I can bathe and clean up a little. We use that door."

Hunter's interest quickened. "Could be that's the time to—"

She didn't let him finish. "The sheriff and the deputy are always with us. And sometimes there are other men. You would only get yourself killed."

He nodded. "That back door—might be that's our best bet. I'll have a look—"

The abrupt thud of bootheels sounded in the office, followed by loud voices.

"That'll be them coming to turn me loose," Jud said. "Been expecting it."

Auralee flung herself against the separating bars, gripped them with her small hands as her eyes widened and filled with tears.

"Oh, dear God!" she cried in a choked voice. "You're my only hope, Jud! Please help me!"

32

4

"What else was it I could've done with him?" Ed Keeter's nasal tone was defensive.

"Had no business starting a ruckus with him in the first place," a deeper voice shot back testily. "Goddammit, Ed, sometimes I wonder about your wearing that badge. You don't never use your head. . . . Now, open up and get him out of there."

The connecting door to the office swung back. Keeter, followed by an elderly, ruddy-faced man—Gosset, Jud recalled Lat Williams calling him—wearing the sheriff's star, stepped into the room. The older lawman stopped short, his features tightening in anger.

"Told you to keep this damned door locked, too! What's the matter with you, Ed?"

The deputy, fumbling with a ring of keys, hung his head. "Reckon I just forgot. Anyways, I—"

"Forgot! Goddammit to hell, your forgetting's getting worse all the time! Said I didn't want nobody else in here while I was holding the Ford woman. You forget and lock up some bird and—"

"Aw, he's just some two-bit saddlebum—"

"That's what you think. Could be he's a friend of hers come to break her out!"

"Don't hardly—"

"Then you trot off leaving both the doors wide

33

open—unlocked! I don't know, Ed. I just ain't sure you got the makings of a deputy."

"Won't happen again, Rufe. I'll sure remember."

Gosset scrubbed at his jaw agitatedly, wagged his head. "Maybe—we'll see. For now, get him out of here. Don't care what you do with him. Lock him up somewheres else or probably best to just run him out of town. Don't make no difference to me."

"Sure—"

"And when you leave, lock the damned doors! You hear? Lock both of them!"

"Sure, Rufe."

"I got to get back to that cattleman meeting Lat pulled me out of."

"Don't you fret none. I'll take care of things right."

Rufe Gosset nodded coldly. "This time see that you do, but I'll drop by in a hour or so, just in case," he said and, wheeling, backtracked through the office to the street.

Keeter remained motionless for a long minute, allowing his ruffled pride to soothe. Then, singling one of the half-dozen keys on the ring, he moved deeper into the room and halted at the door of Hunter's cell. The swelling of his mashed lips had enlarged and there was now a discoloration below one eye.

"Turning you loose," he mumbled as he fitted the key into its lock. "Then you're pulling out.

34

Want you clear of town fast as you can get—understand?"

Jud slid a quick look at Auralee. She was standing close to the bars, eyes bright and hopeful, fixed upon him.

"Them's the sheriff's orders," Keeter was saying. "Me, I'm hoping you don't. I'm hoping you show up around here again so's I'll have a excuse to work you over, square up that little score between us."

Hunter glanced at the deputy's battered features and smiled in amusement.

"You listening?" Keeter demanded, pulling open the grill.

"I'm listening," Jud replied, moving through the doorway.

Abruptly he halted, spun. His knotted fist, traveling a complete arc, caught the lawman on the jaw with all the force he could muster. The impact of the blow slammed Keeter against the bars of the cell. His head snapped forward and the ring of keys dropped from his nerveless fingers as he settled slowly to the floor.

Hunter, moving quickly, jerked the deputy's gun from its holster and threw it across the room into a far corner. He took Keeter under the armpits and dragged him into the cell, wishing as he did there was something readily available with which to bind and gag the man.

But there wasn't and time was a crucial factor.

He stepped to the outside of the cage, closed the door, scooped up the keys and flipped the lock. He then opened Auralee's cell.

"Got to move fast," he said in a clipped voice.

She was out of the cage before he had finished speaking and together they hurried into the adjoining office. He handed her the ring of keys.

"Lock the door while I get my gun," he said.

Wordless, she turned to do his bidding. Hunter, stepping in behind the desk, jerked open the lower drawer into which Keeter had dropped his pistol, recovered it and slid it into the holster on his hip.

"Wait here," he said, and crossed to the entrance of the office.

Standing close to the frame, he glanced up and down the street. A dozen or so persons were strolling leisurely along the walks. There was no one close by. He beckoned to Auralee and as she hurried to his side he took the keys from her.

"We'll step out together. You keep behind me so's I'll block anybody seeing you if they happen to look this way. Walk quick to the corner of the building. Wait there in the passageway for me."

She nodded, frowned. "Did you forget something?"

Hunter grinned crookedly. "Sheriff said to lock this door. Reckon we ought to please him."

They moved out through the door, Auralee careful to stay in Jud's shadow and immediately crossing the front of the jail to the narrow corridor that separated it from its adjoining neighbor. Jud, taking a few moments to locate the proper key, secured the door, stepped back, hesitated. There was a further means for buying a little time; pulling aside, he tossed the ring onto the roof of the adjoining structure.

"We'll need horses," Auralee said as he rejoined her.

"Got mine in the stable behind the saloon," he replied, "but we won't get far riding double. Best I scratch up one for you too."

Jail break, helping a convicted murderer to escape, knocking a lawman cold—and now horse stealing.

That thought drummed through Jud Hunter's mind with dull persistence as they hurried on through the night toward the livery barn. He'd really cut himself into something this time— something that could hang him higher than a kite. But somebody had to help Auralee Ford, give her the chance to prove her innocence, and it had just so happened he was the only one handy.

He shook off his dark thoughts. Likely it would end up all right. Auralee would prove she was not guilty and he'd return the horse he'd just be borrowing for her. That would be it; nobody would get hurt.

They reached the stable of the Kansas Queen, paused at its corner. The racket within the saloon was overriding all other sounds in the street. Hunter was thankful for that; Ed Keeter would come to his senses shortly and start yelling, but with all the noise, it could be some time before he'd be heard. It was best not to plan on that, however. Luck could go against them if someone chancing to pass by the jail heard the deputy's shouts and summoned the sheriff.

"Circle around to the back door," he said in a low voice. "Meet you there."

Auralee pressed his arm, then hurried off into the deep shadows cast by the building. He watched her for a long moment, intensely aware of her being, filled suddenly with a reckless satisfaction at finding himself the one man able to help her, and then moved on toward the stable's entrance.

He could have problems with the hostler—but he'd not let that stop him now, he decided; it was much too late. He was already in deep and there could be no backing off, even if he wanted to. He reached the window of the hostler's office and peered cautiously around its edge through the dusty pane. The stable hand now occupied the cot previously in use by the swamper, Anse, and was sleeping soundly.

Jud crossed to the wide entrance and moved quietly down the runway to the stall where the chestnut was to be. He grunted with satisfaction; the big horse was there. He turned to the head-high wall separating the gelding from his neighbor. His tack was also where the hostler had said it would be, slung over the top board—and the rifle was safely in its boot.

Working swiftly and silently, Hunter saddled the chestnut, backed him into the runway and led him down the straw-and-dung-littered passage toward a square of moonlight that designated the rear door. Reaching that point, he ground-reined the horse and doubled back to the stalls. The first was empty, but in the second he found a bay and immediately stepped in beside him and gave him a hasty going-over glance in the feeble light.

He looked strong and there was no time to be choosy. Pivoting, Jud yanked the blanket and saddle from the wall, and dropped them into place on the animal's back. The kack was an old-style slick tree model with a split seat and double rigging, but again it was a matter of fleeting time; it would have to do. After pulling the cinches tight and buckling the bridle into place, he led the horse to where the chestnut waited. Then, with both, he passed through the back doorway into the open.

He was in a sort of alley that lay between two corrals. In the fairly strong moonlight he could see the crosspieces of a gate at its far end. Once outside that, he would be in the clear and ready to head out for wherever it was that Auralee needed to go.

Quickening his pace, he led the horses down the lane. As he drew near its end, the gate opened suddenly and he saw Auralee waiting for him. He passed through hurriedly and as the bracing of crosspieces swung back into position of its own accord, he handed the reins of the bay to her.

"Maybe ain't much to ride, but he's the best I could do. Expect those stirrups'll be a mite long. I'll shorten them first chance I get."

She gave him a tight smile. "It won't matter. Did you have any trouble?"

"Hostler was sleeping. Won't know I've even been around until he wakes up."

Taking her by the elbow, he boosted her onto the bay. Wheeling, he swung to the chestnut's back. Settling himself, he glanced questioningly at her.

"Which way? Where we headed?"

Auralee faced him squarely. "Mexico," she said in a level voice. "Town called Nogales."

5

"Nogales!" Hunter echoed in a strangled voice.

She nodded slowly, watching him with concerned, apprehensive eyes. In the pale light she was a small, forlorn figure astride her horse, utterly helpless and lost.

"Is it so far?" she asked hesitantly.

"Quite a piece," he answered, and touching the gelding with his spurs, broke him into a slow lope.

He swore deeply under his breath as Auralee moved in beside him. *Nogales!* He hadn't bargained for that. He thought the friends she wanted to see lived somewhere fairly close—one of the ranchers, perhaps.

He glanced at her. She was sitting rigidly upright on the old saddle, elbows stationary at her sides as she rocked gently with the motion of the bay. The moon was flooding her calm features and in its glow they took on a carved, angelic quality.

"Nogales—a long ride," he said as they bore steadily on. "Take ten, maybe twelve days."

"I'm sorry—"

"No need to be sorry. If that's where your friends live, then that's where we've got to go. Plenty of rough country in between here and there—'specially once we get to Arizona. Lot of unfriendly Apaches."

"They'll make no difference as far as I'm concerned," she replied dully. "Hanging or being killed by Indians—it would be all the same. Do you know the way?"

"Been across a few times. Several trails, but I reckon we'd best take the shortest one."

Auralee smiled at him. "I thought you would know. Men like you get around and see everything, go everywhere. I envy you."

He grinned at the compliment. "Not much of a life in some ways, pretty good in others."

Twisting, he looked back toward Prairie City. The noise had long since faded with distance, but the faint glare of its lights, trapped by a hovering layer of dust, was still visible low in the night sky.

"Important thing is to get as far from town as we can quick as we can," he said, resuming position. "That sheriff'll have a posse on our tails mighty fast."

"Being night, won't it be hard to find our tracks?"

"Maybe. Good moon and there's likely somebody handy who's good at trailing. But we've got us a fair start and they'll have to take it slow at first. . . . Just kind of wondering—those friends of yours in Nogales. Being so far off, how can they help prove you didn't shoot your husband? And something else. Nogales ain't such a good town for folks to live in. Could be they've moved."

Auralee was silent for a short time. Then, "A

letter came to me from there, so I know they haven't moved, and being across the border in Mexico, I won't have to be afraid of the law while I'm getting it all straightened out."

"Once we get across the line into New Mexico, Gosset won't be able to touch you anyway. A Kansas sheriff has no authority there."

"But he'll send word ahead—even to all of the nearby states and territories and having them watching for me. Tom Ford will see to that."

"It'll have to go by stagecoach mail unless he sends a rider—and we've got the jump on both. Ought to beat any message easy if we don't run into bad luck." Hunter was quiet for a time. "These folks in Nogales, they know something that will clear you?" he asked.

Auralee stirred on the saddle, nodded. "Everything I need is there and I'll be able to get it all together without being afraid of getting arrested and going back to jail. Tom Ford doesn't have any influence in Nogales."

Hunter made no comment as they pressed on. The country was low, rolling and fairly devoid of brush with only an occasional hill rising above the general conformation of the surrounding land. Shortly he veered left, angling for the nearest rise.

"Need to get my bearings," he explained as she turned quickly to him with a worried frown on her face. "Sooner we get to New Mexico, better I'll feel."

Auralee settled back, satisfied. She rode well, he had noticed, sitting her saddle in the manner of one long accustomed to being on a horse. At least he'd have no problems there.

They reached the foot of the hill, made their way to its summit and halted. Hunter, dropping to the ground, threw his glance to the east. Prairie City was now only a faint glare on the horizon.

"Need to head southwest," he said. "That'll take us across a corner of what some call No-Man's-Land—a sort of a panhandle sticking off one corner of the Indian Territory—and into New Mexico."

"How far?" she asked immediately.

Hunter thought for a moment. "Reckon it'll be about a hundred miles."

"Can we be there by tomorrow night?"

He shook his head. "Horses just ain't in that good a shape—'specially the bay. Doubt if he can stand pushing too hard."

"But if we kept riding—"

"What I aim for us to do. We've got the jump on a posse, want to hold it. Figure to move right along until daylight, then hole up for a few hours."

Auralee looked off across the silvered prairie. "I'll not feel safe until we've reached Mexico," she said in a wistful voice.

"That's what it'll take, sure enough—but we can make it," Jud said, wanting to reassure her. "There's a few trails between here and there most

44

folks don't know about. We'll be taking them."

"I'm not afraid, not with you, Jud," she murmured. "God must have sent you to me tonight."

Hunter grinned. "Maybe so, but I figured it was that right to the jaw I give Keeter back there in the saloon."

Auralee smiled faintly and then abruptly a spasm of trembling shook her. "I was afraid of him. He used to come and stand outside my cell late at night after everyone else was home asleep. He'd just stare at me through the bars. One time I thought he was going to unlock the door and come in. If he had I don't know what I would've done."

He reached up, laid a broad hand upon her wrist. Her skin was cold and he could feel her shaking.

"No need to worry about that now. It's over and done with and chances are you'll never lay eyes on him again." He turned away, moving to the side of the chestnut. He unbuckled the left saddlebag, dug into it and came up with a tightly folded wool jacket, one he ordinarily wore beneath his buck-skin work coat when the weather was extreme. He opened it up and passed it to her.

"Put this on. Gets a mite chilly around here at night and it'll be colder once we hit New Mexico." He paused. "Ought to have a hat too."

He returned to his saddlebags, searched about until he found a faded red and white bandana. She was still struggling into the jacket and he waited until she had pulled it on and buttoned it

45

about her body, then tossed the square of cloth to her.

"Maybe this'll work."

She folded the bandana into a triangle, covered her head with it, securing two of the corners under her chin.

"It will do fine," she said. "I didn't have any of my things. When the sheriff came to the ranch for me he wouldn't let me take anything except what I was wearing—and this." She lifted her arm, displayed the reticule hanging from her wrist. "Not much to start a long trip with."

Hunter crossed to the chestnut, slid a toe into a stirrup and swung to the saddle. His face was sober. "Like to think we could settle our other problem that quick and easy."

"Other problem?"

"Water and grub. We're plumb shy of both and there's no chance of getting any for quite a spell. Reckon we're going to be doing a little thirsting and starving for a while."

Auralee's small, square shoulders moved a trifle. "We can make it. I'm out of that jail and free of Tom Ford. That's all that counts."

Jud Hunter considered her thoughtfully for a long breath and then, nodding, gently roweled the gelding.

"Yeh, sure," he said as he moved off the hill. "Best we be getting along."

6

They rode on across the moonlit flats, picking their way between the low hills, following out the narrow washes, always choosing the easiest route in order to conserve the strength of the horses. Off in the distance they could hear coyotes barking and once a wolf howled from a dark grove as if challenging their right of passage.

Their lack of food and water troubled Jud Hunter greatly, not so much for himself—going without was far from a new experience to him—as for Auralee, who likely had never wanted for anything. There would be homesteaders and ranchers in the area, he knew, and supplies could be obtained from them, but he was reluctant to turn to that source.

Putting in an appearance would immediately establish their whereabouts and be of great help to Gosset and his posse, who would be scouting the vicinity and asking questions of everyone. It was only wise to keep the lawman in the dark as long as possible, force him to rely upon tracking, necessarily a slow process, and thus permit the two fugitives to cover a maximum amount of ground before halting. Perhaps they would find a creek that had not gone dry, although it was late in the summer to hope for that. Meanwhile, he'd keep an eye out for a rabbit.

The hours wore on and by daybreak, which brought a sharp cold that bit deep into their bones, they had reached the edge of the flat country and were entering a broken land of buttes, brush-filled arroyos and long, sandy slopes.

Hunter glanced at Auralee. She was near exhaustion but had uttered no complaint. Admiration stirred him. Auralee Ford was a man's woman, for beneath her veneer of beauty there was a toughness, a strength—like steel clothed in a wrapper of delicate lace.

"We'll pull up over there," he said, kneeing the chestnut in close to the bay and pointing at a thick stand of brush edging the foot of a hill.

She turned to him anxiously. "Do we dare? I'm not the least bit tired."

"Horses need rest. Won't hurt you none either."

Auralee shrugged, swung the bay onto the path set by the chestnut and rode toward the slope.

Hunter guided his mount into the center of the brush and dismounted. Wheeling at once to the girl, he extended his hands and lifted her from the saddle and set her gently on her feet.

"Have to forget about a fire," he said, tugging loose the blanket rolled behind the cantle of his hull. "Put this around you. It'll keep out the chill."

She caught the woolen cover by its edge, draped it over her shoulders and about her body, cuddling it to her gratefully.

"You've nothing to warm you—"

"Won't need anything," Hunter said, jerking a thumb at the crest of the hill behind him. "Taking a walk to the top. Want a look at our back trail."

Fear came into her eyes at once. "The posse—do you think—"

"Don't think nothing special."

"Then why are you going up there to watch?"

"Just something I figure I ought to do, I reckon. Not much chance of them being close to see even if they've picked up our tracks. Always feel better when I'm dead sure of what's going on."

Auralee smiled, expressing her understanding, and moved away from him. She found herself a cleared place in the growth, sat down and leaned back against a sandy ledge.

Sighing, she asked, "How long can we stay here?"

"Noon, or thereabouts. Want to rest the animals good. Might have to travel fast later on. . . . Get yourself some sleep."

Turning about, he led the horses onto a level spot in the brush and, after loosening their cinches, headed up the slope to the mass of rock he had noted earlier. From there he should have no difficulty looking back over the route they had taken.

He gained the outcropping, worked himself forward to its highest point. For a long quarter-hour he studied the gray-brown carpet unrolling before him, probing not only the course they had followed but the country to either side. There were no riders to be seen.

Satisfied, he pulled back into the rocks and settled himself into a comfortable position. He could use a few winks of sleep, too, he realized, and tipping his hat forward to shut out the increasing glare, he closed his eyes.

A time later he roused. The sun was well up and on its way across a cloudless sky. He'd slept two or three hours, he judged, and the break had served him to good purposes.

He rose and returned to the high point and placed his attention to the northeast, again scanning the long flats, now glistening in the strong light, with minute care. The land was empty. Nothing moved except half a dozen buzzards soaring effortlessly above the vast stretches far to the north. That was good. Rufe Gosset and his posse had been shaken even before they had gotten started. It shouldn't be too hard to keep out of their way in the future.

Pleased with the thought, Hunter cut back through the rocks and started down the slope, walking quietly so as to not disturb Auralee. Almost at the bottom he halted. The girl was awake.

She had put aside the blanket and jacket and was standing in the center of the clearing near where they had halted. The flowered bag she carried hung from a close-by sage branch while she touched at her features with a small fold of lamb's wool upon which there was rouge.

There in the strong, driving sunlight Jud Hunter had his first good look at her. Beauty was not confined only to her face; she stood erect, her figure clean-lined and perfect beneath the clinging dress she wore. Her hips were smooth and gracefully rounded, rose to a slim waist that appeared so small he was sure he could encircle it with his two hands, tapered upward to flare into high, full breasts. She had removed the bandana from her head and her hair, deep, rich brown, had a glowing sheen.

Hunter took a sharp breath. He reckoned he was a better judge of horseflesh than of women, but to believe this woman was capable of murder was pure foolishness.

He resumed the descent, no longer taking care. She heard him and turned quickly. Another surge of admiration rolled through him. Despite the circumstances she had taken time to refresh her face—a faint shadowing below the eyes—which were blue, as he'd thought; a redness to her lips and a creaminess on her cheeks.

She greeted him with a quiet smile. "I know I looked a sight. I hope I've improved some now."

Jud wagged his head. "Never figured you could make yourself prettier'n you are," he said awkwardly.

Auralee smiled again and her eyes, taking on

the brilliance of the sky beneath their dark full brows and lashes, seemed to dance.

"I take that as a fine compliment, Jud. Thank you."

He swung about, feeling like a schoolboy, and made his way to the horses. Both appeared to be rested and ready to go—and he could see no good reason not to move on. Every mile gained on the posse was to their advantage.

He tightened the cinches, took up the reins and led the mounts to where she waited. She had completed her ministrations, had tied the bandana about her head again and was folding the blanket. He took it from her, doubled it into a small square and, not taking time to secure it in its usual place, stuffed it into one of the saddlebags.

"I might as well carry the jacket," she said, hanging it over her forearm. "Are we leaving now?"

Hunter nodded. "No cause to wait. Horses are in good shape."

He helped her onto the bay and climbed aboard the chestnut, feeling curiously subdued. They rode out of the brush and, with the sun at their left shoulders, struck off across the irregular land. Shortly she veered in to his side.

"Jud, is there something wrong?"

He glanced at her, shrugged. "Nope, nothing."

"I thought I might have said something or done something to offend you."

Again his shoulders stirred. "Nothing like that. Reckon it's just you—the way you look."

Auralee laughed, a light, happy sound in the broad quiet of the slopes. "Why, that's another compliment! Thank you once more."

"The truth," he mumbled, and spurred on ahead.

They pressed on, moving steadily as the sun climbed to its zenith, began its long slide toward the smoky hills far to the west. Late in the afternoon, during one of the periodic halts made to breathe the horses, he pointed to a long line of bluffs still far ahead.

"There's a town near there, I recollect. Can get us some grub and water. Expect you're plenty hungry and thirsty."

"I am," Auralee admitted. "Will we spend the night there, too?"

"Can't risk that—and I'll have to figure how to get that grub. Don't have a penny on me. Suppose I could sell my rifle."

She brushed wearily at her eyes. "I wish I could help. Seems all I've done so far is make trouble for you. I've mixed you up in my problems, got you in bad with the law—and now you're about to sell your gun so that I can eat."

"Won't be the first time I've bargained it off," Hunter said, and put the chestnut into motion again.

"But aren't you likely to need it? You said something about Indians—Apaches."

53

"Long as I've got my forty-five we'll be all right."

It was full dark when they reached the ring of short hills that overlooked the settlement. The afternoon's heat had been intense and the absolute need for water was now making itself felt. He must find relief not only for Auralee and himself, he realized, but for the horses as well.

Jud dismounted and squatted on his heels, trying to recall what he knew of the town. There was no river nearby—indicating that the inhabitants depended upon a spring for their water supply. The more well-to-do people would have wells.

Either way, it would be necessary for him and Auralee to enter the settlement—one thing he had hoped to avoid. Anyone seeing a man and woman passing through would have the answers to the questions Rufe Gosset would ask when he arrived. A man alone would probably go unnoticed.

"We'll hold off 'til the place closes up and then move in," Hunter said, coming back to Auralee's side. Reaching up, he lifted her from the saddle. "Might as well take it easy. Be a couple more hours."

Side by side on the crest of a hill, they watched the town, seeing the yellow squares of windows wink out slowly, gradually, one by one. When all were dark and only the silver shine of moonlight and the lamps of a solitary building—a saloon, likely—were all that remained to mark the location of the settlement, they mounted and rode quickly down to its edge.

"Wait here," Jud said, slipping from the gelding. "I'll see if I can spot a horse trough close by. Then you can take care of the animals and fill the canteens while I get the grub."

He moved off into the shadow of the first building, returned almost immediately.

"Running into luck," he said, handing her the reins of the chestnut. "There's a trough straight ahead—in front of that old stable. It's empty and there's nobody around. You see to the water, I'll meet you back here."

Auralee leaned forward, caught him by the arm. "Take care, Jud."

He grinned at her through the half-dark. "Goes for you too. You hear somebody coming, leave the horses and duck out of sight quick. Can always scare up something to ride if I have to—but there's only one of you."

"And of you," she murmured as he faded into the night.

7

Hunter, keeping close to the front of the abandoned livery barn, started down the street. He had left the rifle behind, deciding at the last moment not to offer it for sale or as barter in the interests of leaving no trace of their presence in the settlement at all. The less Sheriff Gosset learned, the better.

The faint jingle of his spurs halted him. He reached into a pocket, pulled out two matches, bent down and wedged the small sticks against the star rowels to silence them. Straightening up, he continued his slow walk, glance-searching for the general store along the facades of the half-dozen or so structures that made up the town.

The open doorway of the saloon on the opposite side of the street and a few paces farther down laid an oblong of dim yellow light on the dust. A figure abruptly filled the opening. Hunter froze behind a thick-trunked cottonwood. The man, unsteady on his feet, hesitated briefly, then stepped uncertainly out onto the small landing that fronted the name-less establishment and down into the roadway.

He halted again, apparently unsure of his directions. Hunter frowned, seeing him turn toward the upper end of the settlement where

56

Auralee waited with the horses. A moment later relief filled him. The fellow, finally getting himself organized, reversed his position and, staggering badly, headed for the opposite end of town.

Where the hell was the general store?

Impatient, Jud again scoured the fronts of the structures along the street. His attention halted upon a fairly large, windowless and abandoned building somewhat apart from the others. Straining his eyes, he made out the barely legible sign across its face: T. MASON GENL. MCHDE.

Hunter swore softly. The place was out of business just as was the livery stable. Evidently prosperity was no companion of the settlement—but there would have to be a supplier for those who still lived in the area.

He moved on, halted again as his probing gaze came to rest on the windows of an ordinary house a short distance beyond the saloon. There was no sign, but moonlight striking through the glass panes revealed lines of shelves on which was merchandise. Hunter grunted with satisfaction. The storekeeper, probably to avoid costs, had set up shop in the front quarters of his own home.

Walking hurriedly now, Jud continued along the street until he was beyond the splash of the saloon's lamplight, crossed over and doubled back to the structure housing the store. Sweeping the street with a glance to assure himself that it was still deserted, he stepped up onto the landing, quietly tried the door. It was locked, as he had expected it would be, but he tested it nevertheless on an outside chance that it could have been left open.

Immediately he doubled back to the side of the building, drew up to one of the ordinary-sized windows that faced the south. Pressing his palms against the sash, he pushed upward. It gave a half-inch, checked. Hunter again swore. It too was locked—just as all other windows in the place would be. He drew off to think, hearing the far-off barking of a dog, the rumble of conversation in the saloon.

The saloon . . . There would be little legal difference in holding up a saloon and robbing a store; he'd be breaking the law in either event, as well as leaving proof for Rufe Gosset and his posse that Auralee and he had been there. But it was grub he was after, not money; taking a few dollars from the patrons and the owner of the saloon would not solve the food problem. The only answer was to get inside the store, somehow.

He turned and worked his way along the side of the building to its rear. The merchant maintained living quarters in the rear, that was evident. At this hour he and his family would be sleeping. . . . By being careful—

Quickly Hunter retraced his steps to the window and, drawing in close, he examined the top of the lower sash. It was secured by a simple thumb lock. Glancing about once more to be sure he was alone, he drew his pistol, and using the butt as a hammer, tapped the glass above the lock until a small, jagged section broke free. The noise seemed overloud to him and when it was done he hung there, motionless against the wall, listening.

The murmuring inside the saloon did not cease, nor did he hear any sound or see the sudden flare of a lamp inside the store. The breaking glass had aroused no one. Holstering his weapon, he stuck his fingers through the opening, pressed the circular catch aside, raised the window and crawled through.

He drew up just inside, again listening for any sign of a disturbed owner. There was only a deep silence filled with the mingling odors of coal oil, leather and a spice of some sort.

Time was slipping by. He'd already taken longer than he should and Auralee would be starting to worry. At once he moved deeper into the cluttered room, going first to the counter that stretched across its width at the rear. Squatting behind the benchlike affair, he found what he expected to be there—the storekeeper's supply of empty flour sacks.

He took one and started along the shelves, dropping into it cans of peaches, tomatoes, paper containers of biscuits, packages of salt, sugar, dried apples, several handfuls of potatoes and any other item that caught his eye that would be practical to prepare on the trail.

The end of the shelving reached, he paused to think. Coffee . . . He glanced around, located the mill. The beans were in a large tin alongside. He scooped out a quantity and dumped them into the flour sack; later, when there was more time, he'd put them in a container of some kind.

Bacon—and bread. He crossed to the north side of the store, searching for the window box in which storekeepers generally stored meat. Locating it, he helped himself to a half side.

Bread—it was in a glass case at the end of the counter. Evidently the owner's wife did the baking; the loaves were fresh and he took several, along with a square of cake covered with chocolate icing. Both would be in a hell of a shape by the time he and Auralee could eat, but being mashed wouldn't hurt the taste any.

Halting behind the counter, Jud mentally checked the supplies he'd accumulated. He could think of nothing he'd overlooked except, of course, the paying for them. That realization set up a disturbance within him; add to jail breaking and horse stealing—robbery. He had turned himself into an outlaw fast. But it was all for good cause and later he'd square it with all those involved.

Auralee's proving her innocence would excuse the escape and his overpowering Ed Keeter, who wasn't looked on very favorably by Gosset anyway. He would return the bay to its owner and at the first opportunity drop by the store, explain the situation to the proprietor and pay for what he had taken. Everyone would be satisfied and his brief, unintentional career as an owlhoot would end with no one hurt.

Slinging the sack of groceries over his shoulder, Jud started to turn for the window, paused. A man in a long white nightshirt and holding a shotgun in his hands was standing directly behind him.

"Who're you? What do you want?"

At the demand Hunter reacted instinctively. He lunged to one side, swung the sack of canned goods and other articles at the storekeeper's head. It struck solidly, drove the man against the wall. The scattergun roared deafeningly, filling the room with a blinding flash of light and a surging cloud of smoke.

Jud leaped toward the window as the man collapsed to the floor amid the clatter of falling tins dislodged from the shelves, and the bouncing echoes unleashed by the discharge of the weapon. Reaching the opening, he tossed the sack through and dived after it. He could hear a woman screaming somewhere inside the store as he struck the ground.

Snatching up the precious supplies, Hunter hesitated. The racket would have been heard in the saloon as well as elsewhere along the street; best he return to Auralee by some other route.

Picking up the flour sack, he legged it for the rear of the building, halted at the corner and peered cautiously around it. Two men were trotting toward the street, coming from a small scatter of houses that stood a short distance west of the business buildings. Dogs were barking frantically and lights were coming on in windows everywhere.

Waiting until the men had time to reach the street, Hunter broke into a run, raced along backs of the structures until he reached the last. Breathing hard, he drew in behind a clump of rabbit bush and threw his glance across the way. In the clear moonlight he could see the water trough, but there was no sign of Auralee and the horses. Moving forward until he was on line with the street, he again stopped.

Lights were bright everywhere along the storefronts now, and in the building where he had obtained the supplies and been forced to knock out the owner, he could see several persons moving about. Half a dozen men stood in front of the saloon conversing with the bartender who was filling the doorway with his aproned bulk.

"Auralee!" he called softly into the night.

"Over here."

Her reply came at once from the dense shadow of the abandoned stable. Taking a last glance down the street to be sure he would not be noticed, Hunter crossed over.

8

They rode hard for the first hour, Hunter leading the way on the chestnut, taking a due west course that carried them deep into rough, hilly country. Slowing finally when they were in a sandy arroyo, he turned to Auralee.

"Was a mite close—"

Anxiety still showed on her features. "I was so afraid. When I heard that gunshot I thought you—" She broke off, shivering visibly.

"Man blew a hole in the wall—about all it amounted to. Anyway, we got some grub."

He pulled the flour sack up, rested it on the horn of his saddle. Reaching in, he drew out the cake. Grinning, he handed the misshapen mass to her.

"Brought you this. Hadn't figured on using it for a club, but I reckon the eating ain't been hurt none."

She took it from him, stared at it for a moment and then began to laugh. "A cake!" she cried. "What better time for a cake!"

He continued to smile at her, enjoying her merriment. "Work on it for a spell. It'll hold you until we can stop. Want to get as far from that town as we're able before we pull up."

But the damage had been done, he knew, as they loped on. Rufe Gosset would know they had been there, would be certain it was he who had robbed the storekeeper. Jud had hoped not only to complete the task without detection but that possibly the theft would go unnoticed for several days, but this hope had been killed by the unexpected appearance of the storekeeper. But it was all spilled milk now and there was nothing to be done about it.

New Mexico could not be too far in the distance anyway. There was a row of black-faced lava beds that more or less paralleled the line of division, he recalled, staring ahead. Once beyond that landmark he and Auralee would be free—at least from Kansas law. Despite the brightness of the moon he could not distinguish the formation, however.

With the coming of daylight he breathed a sigh of relief and, turning to the girl, pointed to the dull black scar of flat-topped mesa now behind them.

"That's where New Mexico begins," he said.

Her eyes spread. "Then we're safe!"

"From Gosset and his posse, anyway. . . . Might as well pull up here, fix ourselves a decent breakfast."

He headed the gelding into a small cove in the bank of the wash where an overhanging cedar would throw a small circle of shade and halted. Auralee was off her horse at once, anxious to help. He handed her the flour sack and a long-bladed skinning knife that he drew from inside his left boot.

"Find some bacon in there. Trim us off a few slices for a starter. Can fix whatever else that suits your fancy." He shook his head. "Likely be quite a mess, considering, but expect it won't hurt none."

"It won't," she replied. "Is there something to do the cooking in?"

He stepped to the opposite side of the chestnut, unbuckled the saddlebag and dug out a blackened spider, a small soot-streaked coffeepot, a tin cup, plate and two spoons.

"All the eating gear I've got," he said, placing them on a nearby rock. "I'll get a fire going while you start fixing."

He led the horses off a short distance, picketed them to a clump of brush, made them comfortable and then began to search about for completely dry wood that would create little smoke. Even though the danger of pursuit by Gosset was now past, he still felt it prudent to keep their whereabouts unknown.

They made a breakfast of fried bacon, warmed bread, canned peaches and black coffee. It was far from a feast, but it satisfied their hunger and they rode on an hour or so later promising themselves a complete meal that evening when they would stop for their first good camp.

The advantage was all theirs now, Hunter

believed. With ample supplies of food and water, they could keep to the badlands, far off the regular trails. Also, they were in country with which he was thoroughly familiar and he could plan a route to take them by dependable springs and rivers where there would be ample water and grass for the horses.

Near noon they halted at the base of a towering butte to rest the animals and ease their own muscles. Sprawled in the shade of the formation, Hunter watched Auralee go about the business of rearranging the sack of food, collecting the loose coffee beans, putting them in a paper container that had held biscuits, wrapping the bacon in a cloth she found in his saddlebags and doing other small chores.

She worked in a calm, efficient manner and, studying her, he marveled at her appearance. Despite the long hours in the saddle, the dusty, sometimes hot, sometimes cold miles, she still looked fresh and clean. Only the dress she wore was showing signs of travel.

Auralee felt his gaze upon her, turned to him with a half-smile. "Am I doing things all wrong?"

He shook his head. "Nope, you're doing fine. Was just watching you."

She brushed at something on her sleeve. "I'm beginning to look a sight, again."

"Fact is that's what I was thinking—that you

don't. Hard to see how you manage. Been a tough ride from Prairie City."

"I suppose it's something every woman learns—how to make the best of things. My mother was that way."

"Where is she now?"

"Dead. Since I was about fifteen. My father too. He was killed in the war."

"Recollect you mentioning New Orleans. That where you were born?"

"No, I went there to live after my mother died. My real home is Maryland—a little town near Baltimore."

"Long way from there to New Orleans."

Auralee nodded thoughtfully. "A very long way. A friend took me there, a man who knew my mother. He looked after me."

Hunter gave that a few moments' consideration, disturbed by the meaning that lay beneath her words.

"He still there?"

"He's dead. Someone killed him with a knife. It didn't matter to me. He wasn't a kind man and I was better off. Not long afterwards I got a job dancing in a gambling house. That's where I met Emory."

"And you got married and came here—to Kansas, I mean."

"Yes, and it was all so nice, so different," she said dreamily. "I loved it. Everything was quiet, sort of lonely, actually, but I didn't mind. And Emory wanted so much for me to like it all and be happy. I really was and I think he was happy, too, only Tom was always spoiling it."

"Still got the feeling he was jealous."

"Perhaps. I just know he made it awfully hard for Emory—for both of us. And the hired hands all sided with him, which made it worse. It was like living among a lot of unfriendly strangers."

"You think Tom bushwhacked Emory?"

Auralee opened her reticule, took out her handkerchief and dabbed at the moisture on her cheeks. "I don't know. It's possible. I think he hated Emory that much—and he wanted the ranch for himself. If he didn't do it, he could have had it done."

"How'd it happen?"

"Emory and I were riding. There's a creek that cuts across one corner of the ranch and we'd go there every so often for a little picnic or maybe just to sit by the water. It was a sort of favorite place of Emory's and we started going there as soon as it was spring.

"This time—it was only a couple of weeks or so ago, but it seems like years—we were riding through the willows that grow along the bank. We stopped. Emory was pointing to some birds—summer ducks, he called them—that were swimming about. Then I heard a gunshot. Emory just folded over and fell off his horse."

Auralee paused, looked off across the flat. After a moment she said, "I was so surprised that I didn't realize for a bit what had happened—that he'd been shot. When it finally dawned on me—I guess it was only a few seconds, actually—I got down and knelt beside him. He was already dead. Someone said later that the bullet had gone straight through his heart."

"You didn't see anybody or hear a horse run off?"

"No, not a thing."

Hunter scooped up a handful of sand, allowed it to trickle through his fingers. "Must've been plenty hard on you."

"It was—terribly. I couldn't lift him to get him back on his saddle, so I rode to the ranch for help. I saw right away that they didn't believe me when I told them how he'd been shot—especially Tom. Then, the next day after the funeral, the sheriff arrested me and took me to jail.

"A judge came down from somewhere and they held a trial, found me guilty. I tried to make them believe me, but I couldn't. Everything went Tom's way and nobody would listen. I was so completely alone—no friends or anyone. You see, I'd only been there a few months and Emory and I hadn't gotten around to paying calls on the neighbors and getting acquainted. . . . It was terrible—terrifying, facing all those men, feeling so alone and helpless."

At the break in her voice Hunter stilled the question that formed on his lips concerning the friends she had mentioned, rose and quickly stepped to her side. Laying a hand on her shoulder, he said, "That part's all behind you now. Done with."

She looked up at him, eyes soft and moist. "Yes, thanks to you, Jud."

He grinned, reached down for the sack of food and turned to the horses. "Ought to get cracking, I expect. Know a good place for camp that we can make by dark if we shove right along—trees and a spring and plenty of grass for the horses."

"Oh, that sounds wonderful!" Auralee cried, her mood brightening instantly. She scrambled to her feet. "Maybe I'll even be able to take a bath."

"No reason why not," Jud said, and helped her to the saddle.

It was yet a few minutes before sunset when they reached the small cluster of trees Jud had in mind. The pool below the spring was low due to the lateness of the summer, but the water was clear and cold in the shade of the thickly leafed cottonwood and wild cherry trees, and grass was green and plentiful. For the first time since the start the horses would have good grazing.

Auralee and Jud prepared a complete meal, hurrying to get it over with before darkness fell. Afterward Hunter strolled to the crest of an adjacent hill for a look across the wild, lonely country over which they had just ridden, and Auralee treated herself to a bath in the spring.

When night came he returned to camp, found her wrapped in the blanket, her dress and other things she had taken the opportunity to wash drying on sticks placed around the fire.

"I feel—well—almost new," she said as he stepped into the flare of light.

"Too cold for me," he replied, smiling. "I'll wait for Arizona. Water's a mite warmer down there."

He moved off, began to drag up several logs for the campfire. It was high country and the chill that settled in after the sun vanished was biting and would grow much more intense before daylight.

"Meant to ask you back up the way a piece when we were talking about Emory and when he was shot. You said there wasn't anybody around. How can these friends of yours help if they weren't there?"

Auralee stared at him fixedly for a long minute and then shrugged. "I'm not really sure. They know something about Emory and Tom that will make a difference. Just what it is, I can't say."

Jud shook his head, still not understanding. He lifted one of the logs and laid it across the flames. "Only got that one blanket. Should've thought to grab up one of those back there in the

Prairie City jail, but it never came to me. You use it. I'll hunker down here close to the fire."

Auralee considered him with a quiet smile. "No need for that," she said coolly. "This blanket will be enough for both of us."

9

Morning found them on the trail again, now slicing diagonally across the vast majestic land that was New Mexico, pointing for its deep southwest corner, where they could cut through the Peloncillo Mountains and quickly reach the Mexican border.

There were few words spoken during the breakfast meal, each seemingly lost in a world of secret thought, even fewer once they were underway. But later, as the hours warmed with the climbing sun the silence thawed and they were again passing remarks, the constraint laid upon them by the previous night finally gone.

"You've never told me about yourself," Auralee said. "You've made me do all of the talking."

Hunter shifted on his saddle, pointed to a broad-winged golden eagle plummeting earthward which he was watching. The huge bird dropped from sight briefly behind a brush-hedged crest, reappeared, climbing laboriously into the clean sky, a limp bit of gray fur clutched in its talons.

"Meat for her little ones," he said, looking toward a distant butte. "Likely's got a nest over there."

"Everything has a home, it seems," Auralee murmured wistfully.

"Natural, I guess. Don't count much with some, however."

"Not with you?"

Jud brushed his hat to the back of his head, leaned forward to rest the muscles of his back. "Never gave it any amount of thinking. Not sure I could ever stay put in one place."

"Have you always been one to just ride—drift from place to place?"

"About how it's been."

"Why? There must be a reason, some attraction that keeps you on the move. Is it that you like to see new places?"

He rubbed at his jaw with his right hand, frowned. "No, don't reckon it's that. Found out a long time ago that where you're going always turns out to be pretty much like where you've been. Seems there's just something inside me that wants to keep moving."

"Well, it doesn't make sense," Auralee declared, expressing the resolute incomprehension a woman has for a footloose man. "I'd think you'd want to settle down, have a ranch of your own, raise cattle or maybe horses, have a wife and family."

"Never studied much on that either. Expect it would be a fine thing. A lot would sure depend on the woman—wife."

"It always does, but the man is equally responsible for creating a home—a place where there can be happiness and contentment. I thought I had found all that once, with Emory, but it ended."

Silence fell between them for a time after that, to be broken finally by Auralee. "Where all have you been, Jud?"

"Hard to name. Followed trails all the way from Matamoros to Calgary, working here and there in between. Spent some time in Missouri riding shotgun for a railroad. Left that when things quieted down and traveled west, clear to Oregon. Didn't cotton much to that place. Too cold up there, and always raining."

"And you never saw anything you liked?"

"Sure—this country for one. And Arizona. Both pretty much alike unless you're down Tucson way in the summer. Hotter'n blazes around there that time of year." He hesitated, added, "Never liked any of it good enough to hang up my spurs, however."

"Maybe you will someday."

"Could be. Expect you're finding up here a lot different from New Orleans. Was there once for a few days. Lots of water and grass and trees. Everything all green and pretty as a sage flat after a rain."

"It's another world," Auralee said slowly. "The way people live and do things—it's not the same. There, everyone seems so gay and they think only of parties and riverboats and gambling. Everyone is rich, or makes out like it, and have servants to do the work."

"Even after the war?"

"It didn't change things in New Orleans as much as you might think. A lot of men got rich from it. I guess that's why we went there."

"This friend of yours—was he a gambler?"

Auralee nodded. "A real good one. He was older than I by several years. In fact, he and my mother planned to marry, and then she died. I sort of took her place, I guess. Being alone and so young, I didn't have much choice. But it really wasn't terribly bad and after I got a job at the Golden Horseshoe dancing and singing, I began to meet new people and make new friends."

"Sure would've liked to've seen you then. Bet it was a pretty sight."

"Everyone did seem to like me," Auralee said, smiling. "It wasn't long before I was doing a solo—that means I went out on the stage by myself and performed by myself. The crowd always cheered and clapped. Almost every night some man would send flowers to me and want me to have dinner with him."

"Expect you did, plenty of times."

She gave him a side glance, shrugged. "It was only good business. The more people that came to the Horseshoe to see me, the more money I was paid."

Hunter made no comment. Auralee said nothing for a time, then: "You know, Jud, I think we're very much alike. We're both the kind people call outsiders. I suppose that's why we're getting along so well."

"Could be."

"We sort of have the same needs, except for one, perhaps."

"What's that?"

Auralee fussed with the hem of her dress, one certainly not designed for riding astride, sought to pull it down in order to cover her legs. She met with little success.

"I hope someday to have a real home, have a man I can look up to and love. You don't want to ever settle, stop wandering."

"Expect I could change, was it important."

She turned, looked at him squarely. "Do you mean that?"

His wide shoulders stirred. "Been about everywhere I want, seen most everything I ever figured to. Don't think it would be any big chore was I to find a reason for quitting the trails."

Auralee looked away, stared out across the gradually growing hills. "Could I ever be that reason, Jud?" she asked in a small voice.

He did not answer for a long time. Then, "Expect you'd be about the only reason. Only thing is, I'd have to hold back. Man has to have something to offer."

Her deep sigh was clearly audible to him. "You have plenty to offer—yourself. No woman could ask for more. And far as the rest's concerned, that would soon come. . . . Let's think about it and after we've reached Nogales, and I've gotten everything straightened out, talk it over."

"Suits me," Hunter said quietly. "Know of some land down in Arizona I could get for most nothing. Would make a fine place for a ranch."

"You'd not be sorry?"

"No. Maybe once in his lifetime the right thing comes to a man. He's a fool if he doesn't grab it. That's the way I feel about this—you."

He looked ahead to the jutting brush-studded brow of a butte a short distance to their right. "Horses are slowing up. Time we gave them a breather. Could stand a cup of coffee myself. Be a good spot on that rim to stop for the noontime."

Auralee nodded and together they dipped into a shallow coulee, ascended a flinty slope and halted on the high ground. Hunter swung down, moved to her side and helped her dismount. He checked abruptly, a deep frown pulling at his weather-browned features.

She looked at him, concerned. "What is it?"

"Riders," he said, pointing to a party of horsemen on a distant hill. "Reckon that'll be the posse. Tracker they got must be a dandy. Thing I can't figure is what Rufe Gosset's doing so far out of his territory."

"It's not him," Auralee said in a falling voice. "That man on the white horse is Tom Ford."

10

Hunter's eyes narrowed. "You sure?"

Auralee nodded. "Emory bought the horse for him from a man in Kentucky. Gave it to him a a present when we came from New Orleans. I guess it was a sort of peace offering."

Jud continued to study the distant riders—eight in total. They were too far off to tell much about, but there was no mistaking the carriage and quality of the big white, probably a stallion, being ridden by one of the party; he could only be of blooded stock.

"Do you think they've seen us?" Auralee asked in a tight voice.

"Not yet. That one on the ground, walking about—he's the tracker. Looking for sign right now. Expect I done them a favor when I robbed that store. Put them square on our trail. Hadn't been for that counter jumper waking up and causing a ruckus, nobody'd ever known we passed this way and they'd still be looking for us east of here."

"Don't blame yourself. We had to have food and water."

"Horses were worse off than we were, but no use hashing it over. It's done—and they're there."

"And they'll stay right after us," she finished in

a bitter tone. "I know Tom. He'll never give up until I'm dead."

Hunter reached out, put his arm around her small shoulders and drew her close. "He'll have to walk over me first and he won't find that easy doing."

She nestled against him. "Thank you, Jud. I—I think I'd just give up if it wasn't for you. But what can we do?"

"Keep moving. I'm no greenhorn to this country. We'll cut to the west, get away from the trails, do our traveling in the badlands. It's plenty rough. About the only folks ever going that way are Indians and outlaws dodging a marshal or a sheriff."

"Indians? Won't it be dangerous?"

"Ones up here are peaceable. Only hostiles we'll maybe run into are down Arizona way."

Tom Ford's tracker was still prowling restlessly about. Apparently the posse had picked up the tracks left by the bay and the chestnut in the soft ground at the water trough. Later they had lost the prints and were still trying to find them again. But the general direction of flight had been established and they knew they could not be far off trail.

Hunter realized that from that moment on it would be an absolute necessity for Auralee and him to keep as much under cover as possible. Not only would it be wise to ride deep into the more desolate area of the Territory, but they would need to use extreme care in all they did, avoiding contact with other pilgrims, while taking pains to leave as indefinite a trail as they could.

The man Tom Ford had doing the tracking for him was no fool. He had led the party to the town where the robbery had taken place despite the cold start he had been faced with, and it had not taken Ford long to fit the pieces together once there and the facts assembled. From that point it had been a simple matter for the tracker to locate the sign left by the two horses and move out on a warm trail.

Jud swore silently. In little or no time at all the man had wiped out the lead that he and Auralee had striven to build up. But maybe it was all to the best. They were aware now of the posse and its position, no longer need speculate, and could act accordingly. It was fortunate in a way that they had not known of Ford's presence until after they had obtained the supply of grub and water—even though the need for such had been the main factor in their undoing.

Had they known the posse was so near to them Jud would have bypassed the town, trusted to luck and hoped they could manage to side-track the party and stay alive until they found food and water. It would have been a searing, desperate experience for Auralee with the odds all against winning; he was glad they had not been faced with the necessity.

The tracker was walking back to his horse, either having located the marks he sought or deciding to search elsewhere. At once Hunter dropped his arm from Auralee's shoulders and turned to help her onto the bay.

"Wasting time," he said as she settled herself in the saddle. "Minutes are going to count big from now on."

"What can we do?"

He tried to reassure her with a grin. "Plenty. First off, we're going to lose ourselves in that country you see ahead."

Tom Ford hauled back firmly on the leathers gripped tight in his gloved hand and cursed vividly as he sought to control the fractious stallion. The big white horse had a hard mouth and he disliked stopping and waiting, preferring always to be on the run.

The wrong kind of animal for a working rancher, Ford told himself; one more suited to the race track—but that was Emory for you. He was a great one for doing things wrong, making fool judgments.

Like marrying Auralee. She fitted into ranch life just about as well as sheep mixed with cattle, but you couldn't make him see it. All he could think of after he returned from New Orleans was her, and what time he wasn't in bed with her, he was taking her on rides around the ranch and holding what they called picnics, which really amounted to nothing more than a lot of carrying-on in the grass. Emory had become about as useful on the place as tits on a boar.

Ford swore again, pushed back his hat and wiped the sweat from his forehead with the back of a wrist. A tall, hard-faced man with light hair and nearly colorless eyes, he sat rigidly erect, his mouth a grim, impatient line as he watched Charlie Bull search the ground before them for signs of Auralee's and that drifter's passage.

If the tracks were there Charlie would find them. Half white, half Arapaho, he had grown up on the ranch, adopting the ways and dress of his benefactors but maintaining the cunning and instincts of his red forefathers. He had no equal when it came to following a trail.

"Any luck?"

At Ford's question, Charlie Bull did not look up, only shook his head.

Ford's glance touched on the ranch hands scattered respectfully about him in a loose half-circle and then drifted on to the country spread before them. One thing for damn sure, the girl and her saddlebum friend were out there somewhere—and they'd not get away, not if he had to chase them all the way to hell's harvest! He plain couldn't afford to let her escape that hangman's rope that was waiting for her.

Where would they be headed? Southwest,

generally, it would seem, but that could mean anything: Arizona, Mexico, California, even the Oregon country. He doubted they'd stop in New Mexico; it wasn't far enough from Kansas. California, that would be his guess—and California was a long ride. He hoped they could overtake the pair before the chase extended such a distance, but if they didn't, it wouldn't matter. He wasn't giving up until Auralee was either gunned down out here or back in Prairie City swinging from a rope.

Half-turning, Ford laid his cold eyes on the man to his left. "You stock up on grub back there in Aaronville like I told you?"

The elderly puncher bobbed his head. "Yes, sir, Mr. Ford. Got enough now to last five, maybe six days."

"Good. Be another town somewheres on ahead. Want you to load up again."

"Mr. Ford," the rider at the end of the line said, "how long you figure this'll take?"

The rancher studied the speaker through partly closed lids. "You got something better to do, Earl?"

"No, sir, was only thinking—"

"Don't bother to think. However long it takes, that's what it'll take. We don't quit until I've got that woman."

"What about that jasper with her?"

"What about him?"

"I'm meaning, you aim to get him too?"

"Up to him. He gives us trouble, he's dead. Not letting him or anybody else stand in my way."

The stallion shied wildly as a bird, disturbed by Charlie Bull, whirred suddenly off into the bright sunlight. Ford sawed savagely on the reins.

"Goddam stud," he muttered. "Settle down!"

"Don't hardly seem needful," the rider continued. "Expect he figures he's only helping her."

"Like I said, it's up to him. Can go his way far as I'm concerned, long as he backs off when he see's what's what. Got himself suckered in, which ain't hard to understand. That goddam bitch could hornswoggle the devil out of his tail once she took the notion."

"Here—" Charlie Bull announced, straightening up.

Tom Ford dropped from his saddle, handed the stallion's leathers to the nearest rider and crossed to where the Indian stood. He looked down at the faint scuffing on the hard-baked soil that Charlie indicated. It told him nothing.

"Rode by here," the tracker said. "Were side by side."

Ford's mother had made a personal project of teaching Charlie Bull, while he was growing up, to talk like the whites. There was now very little trace of the blunt Indian gutturalness in his speech.

"You sure it's them?"

The breed squatted, pointed a finger at one of the slight indentations. "It's them. One horse has a crooked shoe. Loose, maybe, and soon coming off. Seen that back in town where they watered. Showed up plain in the mud."

Ford raised his eyes to the weed-and-rock-littered country ahead. "They still striking southwest, you think?"

"Be my guess."

"Guessing ain't good enough."

Charlie Bull shrugged, his dark features impassive. "You want to be sure, then we'd best keep following tracks. Slow, but we won't be making no mistakes."

Tom Ford wheeled abruptly, retraced his steps to the waiting men. Snatching the reins of the stallion from the man holding them, he started to swing up. The horse flung up his head, pulled away, eyes rolling wildly.

"Stand still, you sonofabitch!" the rancher snarled and, grabbing a handful of neck, vaulted onto the saddle. Finding the stirrups with his toes, he settled himself in the big stock hull, then made a quick gesture at the waiting men.

"Move out!" he snapped.

11

Once off the butte Hunter and Auralee pressed hard to cover distance. When the horses began to show the effects of the run, they pulled down to a fast walk, Jud continually scanning the land before them with sharp eyes.

Shortly he found what he hoped for, a rocky slide coming in from the right. Keeping to the same southwesterly course he waited until they were on the storm-washed gravelly surface of the slope and abruptly changed directions to due west. Auralee gave him a hurried look but then, recognizing the move as some sort of strategy, said nothing.

They rode the full width of the slide, veering north as they neared its yonder edge, to reach a long band of densely growing brush. Coming to it, Jud stopped.

"Aim to work through that," he said, pointing at the maze of sage, buckbriar and other stiff-branched shrubbery. "Keep your legs covered. Be some thorns."

He wished he had leather chaps to lend her, but he no longer owned a pair, those he'd had having been sacrificed months previous in the interests of cash for grub.

Spurring the reluctant chestnut forward into

the thick growth, he grinned back at Auralee. "Ford's got himself quite a tracker, but this will set him to doing some head scratching. He'll lose us back there at the start of the slide and he sure won't ever find where we got off."

She smiled, expressing her admiration for his ingenuity. The bay was giving her trouble, however, stubbornly holding back and unwilling to buck the prickly growth.

"Jud—"

He looked over his shoulder again, halted the gelding. The bay was a good five yards behind and unmoving. Pulling on the leathers he forced the chestnut to back until he was within reach.

"Throw me your reins," he directed Auralee.

She flipped the strips at him. He caught them in mid-air and, taking a hitch around his wrist, roweled the chestnut. The big horse lunged forward, jerking the bay into motion. He fought the tight lines for a few moments, neck outstretched, narrow head slanted, and then, surrendering to the steady pressure, caught up. Hunter tossed the leathers to the girl.

"Keep him up close as you can to me. Maybe when he sees my horse breaking trail for him, he'll behave."

The band of brush extended for a good quarter-mile in width, several times that in length as it laid its dark strip along the foot of an extensive row of short palisades. It would be smart to cut a path through the entire distance, but the effort was tiring the horses fast and Hunter figured it was foolish to trade time and distance in any great amount for the sake of hiding their trail.

He began to angle more to the southwest, sighting on another rock-strewn slope that fell away to their right. Gaining its lip, they broke free of the clawing brush and began a slow walk across the curving shoulder. The earth was hard and while there were fewer rocks jutting from its surface than on the previous slide, finding evidence of their crossing would not be easy.

But Hunter was not selling Tom Ford's tracker short. He was better than most, otherwise he'd never have traced them as far as he had. Once he figured out the first graveled slope and the brush spur, he'd start to work on the second. He would eventually find what he looked for, but it would cost the posse time, possibly a full half-day—and Jud knew that time was now the difference in winning or losing.

He gave that thought, wondering at his own choice of words. Win what? Lose what? Did he mean simply reaching the Mexican border ahead of Ford and his posse, or failing to do so? Or was Auralee the prize that filled his mind? He found it hard to separate the two ideas and make the distinction between a contest involving Tom Ford's tracker and himself and the slowly but steadily growing desire to save Auralee and claim her for his own.

Everything had swapped about, it seemed; the woman he had thought only to aid had suddenly become the most important element in his life.

He shook off the perplexing problem, looked ahead. They were going to have to stop to rest the horses. Even the chestnut was lagging after the punishment he'd taken while bulling his way through the tough brush. The bay, a much lighter mount, would be in greater need.

The land angled sharply away to the west and sank into a long arroyo of white sand. A few clumps of rabbit bush and snakeweed spotted its floor, and stunted cedars struggled for life in irregular order along its banks.

He veered the gelding down onto the steep grade and rode into the wash with Auralee bringing the bay in close behind. As he pulled to a halt in the filigree shade of the largest cedar and dismounted, she frowned.

"Do we dare stop?"

"Maybe not so good an idea for us but the horses are beat. Got to give them a couple hours' rest at least. Be a good time to grab a bite to eat ourselves—no fire, just something we don't have to cook and that'll hold us until tonight."

She leaned toward him, allowed him to swing her to the ground. There was a redness along the ridge and on the tip of her nose that matched similar color on the points of her cheeks where the sun was burning her skin. He should have grabbed a hat for her when he was back in that store where he'd loaded up with groceries, Jud realized. If she showed signs of burning worse, he'd insist that she wear his.

He untied the sack of grub and moved in close to the low embankment beneath the tree. Auralee delayed a few moments, fussing with her dress which had become badly twisted during their progress through the brush. Finally satisfied with it, she followed him into the scanty shade. Nearby the horses began to drift off, noses to the dry ground as they sought to graze.

"Do you think we've thrown them off our trail?" she asked, taking the sack from him and rummaging about in its depth for suitable food.

"For a bit. We keep moving for a time after dark we'll make up some of what we lost."

"I don't see how they could ever follow us through that terrible brush, or across those rocks."

"It'll slow them down plenty. . . . Obliged," he added, taking the biscuits she handed him. "How about us opening up a tin of peaches?"

Auralee searched until she found a can of the fruit and passed it to him. He drew his knife, split the top into quarters with two thrusts and folded them back with his thumb. The peaches were in halves, and he speared the top one with the point of the blade and offered it to her.

Auralee accepted it, holding it between her fingers as she nibbled at it. Daintiness of no consequence to him, Hunter managed his portion in two bites.

"Coffee'd taste good," he said, "but we'd be fools to risk a fire. Can set up a good camp tonight, have a big meal and be comfortable."

"The moon will be bright. We could just keep going—not stop."

"Suit me, but the horses would never make it." He glanced at the animals critically. "About done for now. Bay looks like he could cave in most any time."

A worried look came into her eyes. "Maybe we should stay right here—not try to go on at all until morning. If the horses give out—"

"They won't if we handle them right. Thing to do is never push them hard for long in country like this. Stop now and then, let them sort of catch up with themselves. We lay over for an hour now and they'll be good until dark, then with another breather we can move on again. Going to need watering, though."

"We're getting low," she said. "One canteen is empty."

"Be coming to a river in a day or so. Have to make what we've got last."

Reaching into the can again with the knife, he

fished out fresh portions. For a moment he stared moodily at the blade. Then he picked up the flour sack with his free hand and hefted it.

"Getting light, too. Going to need filling again pretty soon."

"Rob another store," she said in dismay. "I hoped we'd have enough so that you wouldn't have to take any more chances—"

"It's get it that way or do some trading, whichever comes handiest. I don't—"

Hunter's words broke off. He lowered the flour sack carefully and came to his feet. Thrusting the knife into its scabbard, he let his hand drop to the pistol on his hip. Auralee, face blanching, rose beside him.

"What is it?"

He shook his head for silence. "Heard something," he replied in a low voice. "Leastwise, I thought I did."

She stiffened. "The posse?"

"Couldn't be them. Were too far back."

"Then who—"

The distinct click of metal against stone coming from somewhere down the arroyo sounded again. Hunter, drawing his weapon, pushed Auralee in behind him and turned to face the noise.

"Don't know, but it sure'n hell's somebody."

12

Tense, Jud Hunter waited, eyes fixed on a brushy bend in the arroyo a dozen strides away. He was certain the sound he'd heard was the striking of a horse's iron shoe against rock. Now, as the slow, dull thud of hooves became audible, he knew he was right.

It could not be Tom Ford and his party. It was impossible for them to have caught up so quickly—but there could be other posses. Hunter's jaw hardened as that thought came to him. The rancher, or Rufe Gosset, might have rushed word ahead directing lawmen of the various settlements to assemble riders and work north in an effort to pocket what they would have termed an escaping killer and her ally. It could be that Auralee and he were finding themselves trapped, caught in the center of a widely flung net.

Jud gripped the butt of his pistol tighter. There was no doubt it could be done. Men riding fast horses, keeping to the hard-surfaced, well-defined roads, could sweep by and beyond the two fugitives, forced as they were to stick to the rougher and necessarily slower trails. By now a warning could have been spread all the way to the Mexican border.

Hunter relaxed slightly. A blue-uniformed soldier wearing the bars of a second lieutenant had appeared at the edge of the brush. Behind him in single file were more soldiers, eight in all. Considering their presence, so far from the populated areas, the odds that they knew nothing of the posse, or posses, were good, but the brittle caution that gripped Jud did not fade entirely.

"Howdy, Lieutenant," he drawled.

The officer straightened suddenly, his youthful features registering surprise. He raised a hand, brought the patrol to a halt.

Hunter slid his pistol into its holster. A bearded buck sergeant, throwing a hasty, silencing look at the troopers displaying their admiration for Auralee in a swell of murmuring and low whistles, spurred forward, to assume a position beside his commanding officer.

The lieutenant, mustering a stern expression, considered first the girl and then Hunter. "What are you people doing here?" he demanded.

"Resting," Jud replied blandly. "You from Fort Union?"

"We are," the officer said briskly, gaze drifting back to Auralee. Nodding to the sergeant, he swung from the saddle. His uniform, while new, carried a fine film of dust, and his polished boots were dull beneath a coat of gray.

"Lieutenant James F. Zimmerman," he said,

stripping off his gauntlets. "Like an answer to my question. What are you doing here?"

Auralee smiled sweetly. "Why, resting our horses, Lieutenant, just as you were told. We're traveling across the country."

Zimmerman looked her up and down. "You don't appear dressed for traveling, ma'am, if you don't mind my saying so."

Auralee frowned, dropped her eyes to the garment she was wearing, brushed indifferently at the front of it. Back in the ranks a soldier breathed gustily and muttered, "Gawd!" in a low, strangled voice.

"Oh, this old thing! I'm just getting some use out of it before I throw it away. I have others."

The officer digested that slowly and nodded. Then, "Traveling from where to where?"

"That army business?" Hunter asked coldly, resentment stirring through him.

Auralee gave him a quick smile, made a small gesture with her hand. "Now Jud, I'm sure Lieutenant Zimmerman doesn't mean to be nosey. He's probably just following orders. Isn't that right, Lieutenant?"

The officer thawed perceptibly. "Yes, ma'am. This is pretty wild country and we like to keep track of folks riding through. It can be dangerous."

The girl's eyes spread anxiously. "Do you mean Indians?"

Zimmerman shook his head, smiled to allay her

apparent fear. "No, ma'am, not Indians. They're all friendlies around here. Only trouble we've had has been in the Pinos Altos country—quite a ways to the west, and that's been a time ago. It's just that folks do die of thirst or perhaps starve if they become lost."

Auralee bit at her lip worriedly, glanced at Hunter and then to Zimmerman. "We are a bit low on water," she said hesitantly. "If you—"

The officer swung his attention to the noncom. "Sergeant, take their canteens, fill them from our supply."

"Yes, sir, Lieutenant!"

"Thank you," Auralee gushed, moving nearer to the officer. "You don't know what a relief that is. Jud will help your man."

Hunter did not stir but continued to watch the girl and the young officer while the resentment glowing within him mounted higher. Auralee was going out of her way to make up to Zimmerman and Hunter found himself not liking it; there simply was no need.

"Canteens—on your saddles, mister?"

The sergeant's question cut into Jud's thoughts. He jerked his head, turned toward the horses with the noncom at his heels. Behind him he heard Zimmerman's voice, pitched low and unnecessarily intimate.

"You're a mighty fine-looking lady, ma'am, if I may be permitted to say so. Would expect to see

97

you traveling in more style—a stagecoach, perhaps."

The chestnut was in front of Jud, the bay a step to one side. He unhooked the canteen and handed it to the sergeant, who unscrewed the cap and began to fill it from one of the several he'd collected from the troopers.

Auralee and Zimmerman had wandered off beyond earshot. Her back was to Jud, but he could see the officer's face, smiling and confident.

"Filled that one," the bearded noncom said, and crossed to the bay. "This here one's plumb empty."

Hunter made no comment. He hoped Auralee, basking in the admiration evinced by the now overwhelmed Zimmerman, guarded her tongue and didn't tell him too much of their plans. That Tom Ford and his posse would encounter the patrol fairly soon was a certainty and the less the officer had to tell the rancher, the better.

"Takes care of that one," the sergeant announced, stepping back.

"Obliged to you," Hunter said, wheeling about and starting toward Auralee and the officer, still engaged in earnest conversation.

"Reckon you wouldn't've had nothing to worry about," the noncom said. "They's a river a half a day's ride to the southwest. Expect you could've made it to there."

"Expect we would," Jud said. He'd like to ask

the direction of the nearest town but discarded the notion. The less mentioned, the less carried to Tom Ford.

Auralee turned to meet him as he came up, smiling prettily, her face flushed from the compliments Zimmerman had evidently been paying.

"You certain there's nothing else we can do for you?" the officer said expansively. "It's our job to help every opportunity we have."

Auralee looked questioningly at Hunter, who shook his head. She glanced again at Zimmerman, held out her hand.

"I guess not, Lieutenant. You've been very kind—and you won't forget the favor I've asked?"

He took her small fingers into his, shook them gently. "I shan't. It's been a pleasure, ma'am."

Releasing her, Zimmerman stepped back, touched the brim of his campaign hat with a brisk salute that also included Hunter, and wheeled to his horse. He and the noncom swung to their McClellans in an identical motion and settled themselves. Zimmerman drew on his gloves, raised his hand.

"Forward—ho!" he ordered with a sweep of his arm and as the small cavalcade of blue moved by he again gave his tribute, but this time his eyes were only on Auralee.

Hunter spun about. He gathered in the reins and led the horses back to where she stood.

"Let's get on the way," he said curtly.

Auralee faced him, a frown puckering her forehead, and allowed him to assist her onto the bay. As he turned to the chestnut she called after him.

"Jud, is there something wrong?"

He cut his mount around sharply, went to the saddle. "You—and that shavetail," he said, heading off down the arroyo.

Drumming the bay's flanks with her heels, she hurried to catch up, her eyes narrowed and thoughtful.

"What about me and Lieutenant Zimmerman?"

"Couldn't see the need for all that cozying that was going on. You tell him what we were doing here?"

"Only that we were traveling through," Auralee said. A faint smile parted her lips. "Why, I believe you're jealous."

He swung the chestnut up and out of the arroyo with a hard hand. "The hell I am! Just worried about what you maybe told him."

He didn't think he was jealous, but he couldn't really be sure, never before having experienced the feeling he had for Auralee. He had resented the way she made up to the officer and if that was being jealous, then he reckoned he was. For some reason, however, he couldn't admit it.

"You tell him where we were going?"

"I had to give him an answer of some kind. I said Arizona."

Hunter grunted, satisfied with that. There was nothing definite about it and it covered a lot of country.

"I asked him if there was a town anywhere near. There is, a half-day's ride on south. We can get supplies—"

Her words trailed off as he turned and, features dark and angry, looked over his shoulder.

"Knew that, but we'll sure as hell have to pass it up now. Ford'll be bumping into that patrol before it's even dark and be asking questions about whether they've seen us. We can figure on the posse being at that town, just waiting for us to show up."

"I hardly think so," Auralee said quietly. "I never told him we were going there. Besides, he'll never tell Tom anything."

"Why not?"

"I made him promise not to mention seeing us if he ran into the posse."

Hunter snorted. "And you don't think he will?"

"He gave me his word—"

"Nothing special about that."

"I think there is with him—or, at least, will be. I told him Tom was my brother, that we'd run off to get married and he was trying to stop us. He wished us luck and said you were a very lucky man."

Hunter swore, lowered his head contritely. "I

sure as hell am," he said. "And I reckon I'm a plain damned fool along with it. I'm begging your pardon for acting the way I did."

Auralee urged the bay forward until she was alongside. Leaning far over, she kissed him lightly on the cheek.

"It's all right—I rather enjoyed it. It's the first time a man's gotten worked up over me in a long, long time."

13

They rode south with the towering snow-crowned peaks of the Sangre de Cristo Mountains laying a formidable barrier to their right, long gray-green valleys and lesser hills on their left. It was high country and there was a crispness to the air despite the unchallenged sun sailing above them in a cloudless blue sky.

The awareness of their need to replenish supplies soon was forward in Jud Hunter's mind, but he was reluctant to visit the settlement that lay within easy reach to the east. Perhaps Zimmerman's word could be relied upon, but there were seven other men in the patrol and any one of them could in casual conversation, awed and impressed as they were by Auralee's beauty, mention having seen them. Such information was certain to reach Tom Ford quickly.

Jud had seen no sign of the posse since that first glimpse, and the knowledge that he had been able to confuse and delay the rancher and his followers was comforting if not wholly satisfying. He would feel complete relief only when he knew definitely that the threat Ford represented to the girl had been removed for good—and that would come only when the Mexican border lay between them.

Near sundown, as they were crossing a wide, open flat, he spotted two riders moving toward them from the east. That they were not members of any posse was self-evident since they were approaching from the wrong direction, and he reckoned them to be only pilgrims enroute to some distant point.

An hour later, with Auralee sagging with weariness, they arrived at a stream, flowing swift and cold in a rockbound channel, and drew to a halt.

"Be a fine place to camp," he said, dismounting.

She shrugged indifferently, smiled wistfully as he stepped up and lifted her from the saddle. "I've almost forgotten what it's like to sit down to a good meal or sleep in a real bed."

"Time'll come again," Hunter said.

"I know that," she said hurriedly, making an effort to shake the apathy that gripped her. Looking around, she nodded. "This *is* a nice place—trees and grass, and that stream."

"Think maybe I can scare up some fresh meat, too. Saw a rabbit over there in the bushes when we rode in. Soon as I picket the horses I'll try snaring him. You get the coffee and whatever else you want ready."

Auralee turned at once to the chore of collecting firewood. Hunter dropped the now depleted flour sack on the ground near her and led the horses off a short way, removed their gear and

104

stationed them where they could graze and water.

He crossed to the place where he had noticed the cottontail, and set a slip-noose snare over the entrance to the burrow, using a strip of rawhide and a stout willow, bowed and held in place by a forked stick, and then retraced his steps to the camp. Auralee had a fire going with the coffeepot, filled with water, already beginning to simmer. She looked at him questioningly. He shook his head.

"Be a few minutes—if we're lucky."

Almost at that same instant they heard the quiet swish of the willow snapping upright, a frantic thrashing among the leaves.

Jud grinned. "Guess we can figure on fried rabbit for supper," he said, and hastened to retrieve their small prize.

Later as they sat in the glow of the warm flames, at ease after a satisfying meal, Auralee turned to him.

"I know we haven't gone very far yet, but how many days do you think we are from Nogales?"

She was thinking of Tom Ford and his posse, he knew. The possibility that the rancher would overtake them was an ever present worry in her mind.

"Not doing bad," he said, hoping to bolster her spirits. "Won't be so hard going from here on. Got maybe eight or nine days ahead of us."

She sighed. "Still a long way. And we'll have to do something about food."

"Figuring on it. Next town we come to will be it. Passed up the one that lieutenant told you about. Scared one of the troopers might do some talking and we can't afford to take any—"

"Hello, the camp!"

At the call, coming unexpectedly from the dark brush beyond the flare of firelight, Hunter rocked sideways, drew his weapon fast and leaped to his feet, with Auralee's startled cry of fear ringing in his ears.

"Ain't no cause for shooting," the voice continued. "We're just a couple of poor cowhands riding west."

"Move out where I can see you," Jud ordered.

There was a rustling in the undergrowth and shortly two men, bearded, dressed in worn denims, faded plaid shirts and badly run-down boots, walked into the glow. The pilgrims he'd seen coming in from the east, drifters like himself—and probably outlaws as well.

"Sure hated to spook the lady," one said, pulling off his sagging brimmed hat to reveal a shock of thick red hair. He had small eyes set deep in a round face, a nose that had been broken. "Name's Kemp. Folks what know me usually call me Red. My partner here's Bud Akin."

All the time he was speaking Kemp had not

taken his gaze off Auralee but stared at her steadily, like a half-starved animal watching its intended prey.

Akin said, "Howdy," in a flat nasal voice.

He looked much the same as Kemp except for being smaller, wirier and with a thick ragged mustache to match the growth on his cheeks and chin. His attention, also, was fixed on Auralee, and Hunter had a quick wonder as to how long they had been standing in the brush watching and listening.

"That there coffee sure does smell good," Kemp said. "Reckon you could spare us a cup?"

He didn't wait for an answer, simply moved into the circle of light while Akin closed in a bit to his left, and, hunkering down, took up the tin cup used by Auralee and helped himself from the pot. His partner, picking up the peach can Jud had converted into a second container, followed suit.

Hunter watched them narrowly. They were testing him, pushing hard to see how far they could go. Evidently they had left their horses back a ways in order to approach quietly and it was clear they had other things in mind than eating or visiting. Neither had expressed any desire for the remaining food in the spider and there was a forced neighborliness in their manner.

A long-forgotten bit of advice given to him in jest by a friend filtered into Jud's mind: *If you ever take the notion to marry up, don't pick yourself a pretty woman 'cause ever horny jasper you meet'll be trying to take her away from you.* He guessed that was what he was up against now. He holstered his weapon and crossed his arms.

"Where you and your man heading?" Kemp asked, grinning broadly at Auralee.

"West," Hunter replied before she could answer.

"Covers plenty of ground," Akin murmured, setting the tin, only half emptied, at the edge of the fire. "How long you been in the saddle?"

"You got some special reason for wanting to know?"

The drifter shrugged, reached into his shirt pocket for tobacco and cigarette papers. "Just trying to be friendly."

"Time for that was when you come skulking in, quiet as Comanches, and sentried yourself there in the brush instead of singing out first off."

"Wasn't meaning no harm," Kemp said, draining the last of his coffee. "Plain joys me to hear a woman laughing and talking, and with yours a setting there like she was with the light kind of shining on her face, was a mighty pretty picture. Anyways, we had to be sure. Man can get hisself shot walking into a camp if he ain't right careful."

"What you can expect if you try it on us again," Jud said coldly. "You've had your coffee. Best you be on your way."

Akin lazily shifted his eyes to Kemp. "He sure ain't very friendly, is he? I figured we was visiting home folks."

Red wagged his head. "Leastwise, he ain't. How about you, lady, you wanting us to go?"

Auralee nodded. She had remained silent from the moment the pair appeared. Gripped by fear, she sat with legs drawn up beneath her, gaze fixed on the dwindling flames.

"Well, now, if that's what you're wanting, that's sure what you'll get. We're nice boys, only maybe a mite lonesome. It ain't often a couple of poor critters like us comes across a looker like you."

Hunter allowed his arms to fall, his right hand to settle upon the butt of his pistol. "Said to move on, don't aim to say it again."

Kemp grinned widely, bobbed. "Yes, sir, mister! We're going right now. Sure don't want to upset you none."

"If you're figuring to camp, pull off a fair piece. Plenty of stream here for all of us—and I get jumpy when I hear somebody moving around in the dark."

"You bet," the redhead said, drawing himself upright and beckoning to his partner. "Come on, Bud, best we let these here folks get to bed. Don't want nobody ever saying we hung around where we wasn't wanted."

Akin rose and stepped back from the fire. Kemp swept off his hat and made an exaggerated bow to Auralee.

"Good night, lady. Was real pleasured meeting you and I'm hoping we'll meet again. Yes, ma'am, I sure do."

Hunter waited until they had reached the brush and then stepped quickly back into the shadows, circled hurriedly and moved in behind them. Shoulder to shoulder, conversing earnestly, the two men were walking toward their horses a scant hundred paces distant.

He remained motionless, watching them build a fire when they reached their camp spot and settle down beside it. They did not remove their blanket rolls from their saddles and, noting that, Hunter turned and went back to Auralee.

She was standing close to the edge of the light, the brightness of fear still in her eyes. As he came out of the darkness she ran to him, threw her arms about his waist.

"Oh, Jud—I'm so frightened! Those terrible men—I know—"

"Never mind," he said, soothing her. "They won't try nothing—not for a bit, anyway. I'll be ready for them."

She tipped her face to look into his. "How? There are two of them—only you, alone."

Hunter shrugged. He had never killed a man, but the probability of being forced to do so was before him now and that realization bred a strange sort of reluctance in his mind. He shook it off. If it was for Auralee's sake, it was for a good cause. Still, if using his gun could be avoided—

"I've run up against their kind before. Expect I can handle them. . . . Want you to take the blanket, find yourself a bed over there by the trees and get some sleep. We'll be moving on in a couple of hours and I've got a few chores to do first."

14

Auralee wrapped the blanket more closely about her body and shivered. It wasn't the cold so much as it was the recollection of how those two men—Kemp and Akin—had looked at her, seemingly stripping her of all she wore as they ravished her with their little pig eyes.

And Jud was worried about them, perhaps even a little afraid, although it had never before occurred to her that he could ever fear anything. Rolling over, she turned her attention to the horses. He had walked off into that direction. She saw he was saddling them, making ready to travel.

They were giving up the camp, moving on. That's why he had wanted her to rest. She felt a sinking within her; Jud was afraid and that sent her own fears soaring to new heights, and then she calmed. She had faced worse moments and come through—and Jud had good reason for taking precautions. They were two to his one, and at night, with darkness to hide them, they could easily overcome him.

He finished preparing the horses. She turned back, again faced the camp. He moved by her, treading softly to avoid awakening her, crossed below the fire, now little more than embers, and took up a stand at the edge of the brush. He was

112

keeping an eye on the men, she saw, and likely would continue to until he decided it was time to go.

After a while he dropped to his haunches and all she could see was the dark silhouette of him crouched there in the night as he maintained his watch. Auralee shivered again, snuggled deeper into the woolen cover. She *was* tired and she really should get some sleep.

A hand shaking her shoulder gently brought her bolt upright. Fingers suddenly pressed against her lips stifled the cry of fear that rose to her throat.

"It's all right," Hunter's voice assured her. "Only me. Time we moved out."

Auralee scrambled to her feet, hurriedly began to fold the blanket. He had led the horses in close and as he turned to help her mount, he nodded at the wool cover.

"Best keep that handy. Going to be cold riding. You'll need it around your shoulders."

She settled herself in the saddle, teeth chattering as the night's chill bit deeper into her body.

"Are they still there?" she asked, drawing the blanket about her as he had suggested.

"Was a bit ago."

She glanced around the camp. It had been an attractive spot at first; now all moonlight and deep shadows, it appeared threatening and dangerous.

"I understand why you think it best we go. There's no way you could protect yourself."

"Never was much hand to take long chances."

"It's me that you're worried about. If you were by yourself you'd not let them drive you off."

"Would make a difference," he admitted, climbing onto the chestnut. "Not about to let something happen that'd get me out of the way and leave you for them. Ready?"

Auralee murmured assent and swung the bay in behind him. He led the way downstream for some distance, getting beyond all possible earshot of Kemp and Akin, she supposed, and then where the banks were almost at a level with the water, forded the stream. They broke out into a narrow valley hemmed in darkly with thick trees. He put the horses to a lope at once, wishing apparently to reach more open country as quickly as possible.

The night was bright around them, changing the grassy floor of the swale into a carpet of faintly stirring silver. Off in the trees a bird called, an owl she thought it was, and over in the low hills in the direction of the mountains the ever present coyotes were yipping their discordant complaints into the hush.

It was easy going and the rocking of the saddle on the bay was like a lullaby and reminded Auralee of the days when she was small—long before the coming of New Orleans and womanhood. That she would one day find herself far off in an only partly civilized land, riding through the night with a rough-cut, hard-edged man she scarcely knew while danger lurked in the background was something she could never have ever dreamed of.

Nor would the thought have entered her mind later when in New Orleans she was having her day as the reigning beauty of the gambling halls and men were fighting to stand beside her, touch her, spread lavish dinners before her while they plied her with expensive gifts. She had lived as a queen, the envy of all the other girls, the toast of men—and she had gloried in it.

But that was the past now, having ended the day she married Emory Ford. The abrupt change was at first a shock and then later, at such a removed distance, she became aware of a relief, a thankfulness, admitting to herself that the crown had begun to fall askew, that the crowd of worshipers had dwindled, attracted to new and younger rivals all blessed with the natural attributes that had stood her in such good stead.

Her day was not really over and gone for all time, however. She could tell that by the way men still looked at her, by the brightening, hungry gleam that came into their eyes, the change in their actions. There were few with the exception of Tom Ford and those beholden to him, and one other, that she could not do with as she willed; some responded fawningly, others with a polite sort of intensity, like Jud Hunter.

And those two back near camp, Akin and the redheaded Kemp. Her effect upon them would have been laughable had the situation not been so dangerous. She stirred, trembled, visualizing herself trapped, being alone with them.

A low word from Hunter brought the chestnut ahead of her to a halt. She reined in quickly, peered forward into the half-light. Two riders were moving in from the dark band of brush and trees to their left. A jolt of fear went through her. It was Kemp and Akin. Evidently they had seen them leave and hurried to cut them off.

"Oh, God!" she moaned softly, unable to control herself.

She watched Hunter, a dark square shape in the night, ease his horse slightly to one side, away from her. Akin and Kemp halted, dismounted, spread apart a short distance away.

"Well, now," the redhead drawled in his derisive way, "we sure didn't figure on you folks jumping up and moving on. No, sir, we sure didn't."

Hunter made no reply.

"Me and Bud here took us a notion to pay you another little visit back there, kind of a sociable one, and danged if you wasn't gone when we showed up."

"Was right disappointing," Akin added, "so we grabbed our horses and rode real hard to get in front of you."

"Be smart. Climb back on them and keep going," Jud said in a voice cold as winter's wind.

Kemp glanced at Akin and laughed. "Now, that ain't exactly what we got in mind. We was planning a little surprise for you," he said, shifting his attention again to Hunter. "Want to know what it is?"

Jud once more was silent. Auralee noted a slight lifting of his right shoulder.

"Well, here it is—me and Bud's decided we're going to take your woman."

The pistol, ready in Hunter's hand, blossomed bright orange—once—twice. The thunder of the accompanying blasts blended almost into one. Kemp went over backward as if struck by some mighty force. Akin spun half-around, fell forward. The chestnut and the bay, startled by the sudden explosions, shied violently, heads bobbing nervously as the echoes rebounded through the night.

Hunter appeared not to notice. He sat rigidly erect in the saddle, eyes on the two figures sprawled below him. Auralee, finally shaking off the paralysis that gripped her, urged the bay to his side. Impulsively she reached out for his forearm.

"Oh, Jud—"

His muscles were tightly drawn, the skin cold to her touch. He seemed caught up in some sort of trance that held him immovable and devoid of feeling. And then abruptly the stiffness went out of him.

"They had it coming," he murmured as if consoling himself, and turned to face her. "You want to cut back to the river and camp or go on?"

He was his old self again, quiet, considerate and, as always, thinking of her. She stilled the trembling in her throat, managed a smile.

"Let's go on," she said.

15

They rode on, now side by side as they entered a vast prairie that gradually opened wider before them. Near daylight they came to another stream, one much smaller than that where they had made the earlier camp, but it was clear and cold and again grass was plentiful for the horses.

In a short time Hunter had a fire going and Auralee a meal underway over the flames. They moved about in silence, often brushing against each other, but no words were spoken, the disquieting recollection of two dead men lying back in a dark and narrow canyon seemingly placing a constraint upon them. But by noon the repression had vanished and the incident, like others of similar, somber nature, had become relegated to the deeper recesses of their minds.

The day had warmed, again one of brightness under a clean sky. They crossed the broad plain, came into a land of small valleys, passed through, found themselves once more on a high plateau as they continued to bear steadily toward the mountains in the west.

Several times they saw herds of white and tan antelopes flashing across a flat, and once, when they came to the rim of a butte overlooking a wide sink, Auralee cried out in delight as she viewed a broad spread of wild asters turning the country almost as far as she could see into a rich tapestry of purple and gold.

There was still no sign of Tom Ford and the posse. At each crowning rise Hunter made a careful survey of the land to the north and east of them but saw no riders, and hope began to grow within him again. Perhaps he was wrong about the rancher; perhaps Ford had given up the pursuit. He was not so optimistic, however, that he mentioned the possibility to Auralee.

Late in the afternoon smoke on the horizon drew their attention. Hunter, mindful of the need to replenish the flour sack larder, altered their course slightly east to reach it. They arrived at the settlement well after sundown, kept a safe distance away while they dined on hard biscuits and the last of the peaches and then, when there were no more lamps alight along the street, they moved in.

Jud dumped what remained of their food stock into one of the saddlebags, left Auralee and the horses at the lower end of the town and made his way along the rear of the two dozen or so structures until he located the general store.

An open window made entry simple and he climbed through. Prowling the shelves with greater selectivity this time, he chose more practical items for the sack, finally concluding the shopping tour with a hat for the girl. His conscience again pained him with the reminder that he was once more committing a theft, but he salved the twinge by promising himself to return and make proper payment—someday.

One thing certain should Tom Ford visit the town: this time he would find no evidence of their passage, for the episode transpired without interruption. Pleased and relieved with that knowledge, Jud returned to Auralee with the saddlebag, presented her with the much needed bit of headgear, and then they rode on.

Well below the town, they halted in a coulee, assembled a meal, ate and slept the remainder of the dark hours. By dawn they were on their way again, slanting now for a pass in the ragged line of a second range of mountains that tailed off the receding Sangre de Cristos.

The subsequent days and nights moved by with a monotonous sameness, brought them finally through the cleft in the frowning rock-strewn hills, down a long slope to the Rio Grande. They forded the wide, shallow stream below a town of fair size, climbed a steep embankment and once more found themselves on a far-reaching plain.

The high hills with their ridges and peaks were now to the left of them as they swung almost due south. Far to the west they could see a solitary towering formation already capped with snow, while up the river a sprawling area of black lava buttes and volcanic cones lay to their backs.

It was much warmer than it had been on the opposite side of the mountains; evidence of this was to be seen everywhere. There was a deep greenness over the land, and the long valley that paralleled their trail was blocked into numerous small farms. Birds were plentiful: horned larks, doves, roadrunners, an occasional shrike, while large coveys of blue-scaled quail scampered regularly out from beneath the horse's hooves. Yellow-blossomed rabbit bush and snakeweed and cottony Apache plume dominated the flats, interspersed here and there with patches of asters, cactus and thick-leafed moonflowers.

Traveling was easy, pleasant, and lulled Auralee into a sense of security and well-being. One evening, halted beside a small spring for night camp, she walked to a low hill and gazed out over the limitless landscape, turned soft amber by the setting sun.

"It's all so beautiful," she murmured, "and everything is going so well. There's been no sign of Tom and we've had no trouble. . . . I'm beginning to dread the day when we'll reach Nogales and this will end."

Hunter, nearby, paused in the process of unsaddling her horse. "Won't need to—not unless—"

"I didn't mean that the way it sounded," she cut in hurriedly. "I meant our being on the trail, just riding along, seeing such lovely things."

Hesitating, she added: "I think I understand you a little better now and why it is you've never settled down."

He turned slowly, swept the land with his eyes, made his appreciating appraisal of its majestic grandeur. At that hour, with the hidden sun spraying the sky with gold, its beauty took on a hushed and mysterious quality.

"Reckon I haven't taken a look at it in quite a spell. Man riding along day after day sort've gets used to it and pays no mind."

"I don't believe I could ever forget a time like this—the sun below the horizon, the quiet that's everywhere."

Far down in the valley a meadowlark whistled cheerfully. Hunter stood listening, strong features impassive. Auralee crossed to his side, put her arm around him.

"I wish it could always be like this."

He looked closely at her. "No reason why it can't, or maybe something about the same. Way I see it, life's just what you make it and I've always had the feeling that since I'm passing through one time, it's smart to do my living the way I want."

"And that's what you've done."

"Tried, for sure. Could be I'll end up flat busted and worth nothing to nobody. Probably will, in fact, but I can always tell myself I did what I wanted to do."

She tightened her grip about him, moved off to start the meal, and Hunter resumed his work with the horses. They ate, seated next to each other while again a strange silence, like a thick wall, fell between them. When the meal was over and the necessary chores dispatched, Auralee sought out the blanket.

"I'm tired tonight," she said in explanation of foregoing their usual time around the campfire talking and drinking coffee.

He only nodded, electing not to question her or intrude upon whatever thoughts were occupying her mind, and a short time later, after building up the fire, he also turned in.

The next day was much like those that had gone before, as was the succeeding night, but near the noon of the one following, their untroubled, idyllic passage came to an end.

Jud became conscious that the bay was lagging, falling behind the chestnut's steady pace. He drew to one side for a better look at the horse and he pulled to a complete halt quickly. The little gelding was limping.

"What is it?"

At Auralee's anxious question he dismounted, pointed at her horse. "He's gone lame. Didn't you feel him holding back?"

She dropped from the saddle hurriedly, worry tearing at her face. "I wasn't thinking—dreaming, I guess."

Hunter stepped up to the bay, rapped the favored leg and examined the hoof. He straightened slowly.

"Thrown a shoe," he said heavily. Half-turning, he looked over their back trail as if hoping to see the lost bit of iron.

"What does that mean?"

"Still a long way to Nogales. Have to get him shod, because you sure can't ride him far with a shoe gone. Chances are the others need changing, too."

"We'll have to find a blacksmith."

"Only answer," he said, studying the surrounding country thoughtfully as he sought to establish their position. After a bit he nodded. "Guess it could be worse. I'm remembering there's a settlement on down the river a piece—about a day's walk. Can light out for it."

16

It was a tough break. Assuming Tom Ford was still on their trail, losing a day could be serious. True, there had been no sign of the rancher and his men, but that could mean nothing; he would have lost considerable time back on the rocky slope and in the dense band of brush beyond it and thus should be hours behind them; now, unknowingly aided by a crippled horse, he would recover lost ground fast.

However, there was still the possibility that Ford had given up and returned to Prairie City—but there was no way of knowing that for sure and Hunter took little comfort in the wishful thought. It was best he play it safe, assume that the rancher and his posse were still following, and plan accordingly. And so they pressed on as rapidly as possible through the warm day, Hunter leading the two horses, Auralee alternately riding the chestnut or walking beside him.

Around midafternoon they broke out of the short hills and halted at a small stream. A quarter-mile farther on they could see the settlement, crouched in a tree-encircled swale.

"Place is called Burnt Pine, near as I recollect," Jud said. "Odds are there'll be a blacksmith there." He glanced over the country to the west.

"You take my horse, follow the creek until you're on the other side of town. I'll meet you there."

Auralee looked down at him worriedly as she settled herself in the saddle. In the driving sunlight her eyes were a brilliant blue. "I—I'm afraid for you to go—show yourself."

"Aim to try and keep from being seen, except by the blacksmith," he said, pulling the rifle from its boot. "Best you keep out of sight if somebody comes along."

She nodded, glance on the rifle. "Do you think you'll have to use that?"

He grinned. "Kind of hard to steal a job of horseshoeing. Figure to trade it."

She smiled and, thumping the gelding's flanks with her small heels, moved off along the quietly flowing stream. Hunter watched her for a time while he considered the words she had spoken. There was risk, of course, in entering the town; Ford could have gotten word to Burnt Pine as well as all other settlements lying between Kansas and the Mexican border, sending it by courier or stagecoach mail. However many of these settle-ments there were, they were not so numerous as to make it a difficult task.

It was a possibility that word had been sent ahead that had prompted Jud's decision to go in alone, sending Auralee on to wait for him a distance away from town. While he disliked the idea of her being by herself, it was certain that any information forwarded by Tom Ford would specify a man and a woman, and their appearance together would unquestionably bring the law down upon them.

His luck was better than he'd hoped for. He spotted the blacksmith's shop, a small structure with an extended canopy, at the near edge of the settlement. It's location would make it unnecessary to show himself on the street.

The smithy, a squat, thick-shouldered, sweating man in overalls and leather apron was working on a big, bucket-footed, woolly-looking black as Hunter led the bay in under the overhang. He paused, glanced up.

"Something you want?"

"Horse of mine threw a shoe," Jud replied. "Expect he ought to be shod all around. You do it right away? I'm kind of in a hurry."

The husky man released the black's foreleg, turned. "Ain't never met the man yet that wasn't in a hurry," he mumbled, and reached for the bay's leathers, hesitating briefly to give the horse a swift, critical appraisal.

"One thing," Hunter said. "Plumb out of cash money. Have to give you my rifle for pay."

The smithy straightened, wagged his head and swore. Glancing at the weapon, he spat, looked momentarily off into the sunlit area beyond his shop, and nodded.

"All right," he said. "Reckon I can come out. Put it there on the bench."

Hunter laid the rifle aside, stepped back to the front of the canopy, eyes scanning the street. Two men were standing in front of a saloon; another was sweeping the landing of a saddlery. There were few stores, and most of them bore no signs. Evidently the proprietors relied entirely on customers who knew of their existence. The marshal's office . . . It stood just beyond what appeared to be a bakery. There was no indication of the lawman's presence.

Jud settled back, resting himself on a keg. The blacksmith was already at work on the bay's off hind leg and would probably attend to the one opposite next.

"You ride him far with that shoe gone?"

At the squat man's question Hunter withdrew his attention from the street. "Just a short ways. Noticed him going lame."

"Hoof's a bit chewed up," the smithy said, again glancing toward the center of town.

Hunter studied the man coldly as suspicion began to grow within him. He seemed much too interested in what lay beyond his shop.

"I'm in a bit of a hurry—"

The blacksmith grunted, resumed his task. After a time he finished replacing the lost shoe and started work on the opposite hoof.

"Where'd you say you hailed from?"

129

Hunter smiled. He hadn't mentioned it and he certainly was of no mind to do so. But the question needed an answer. "Texas'll do."

"Headed for Mexico?"

"Could be, and could be Arizona or maybe California."

"Lot of folks going out there. Can't see why. Gold petered out a long time ago. I—" The smithy drew up slowly, his small, sharpy eyes reaching to the street beyond Hunter as satisfaction spread across his lined features.

Jud pivoted. A tall graying man, angular as a stork and wearing a town marshal's star, was standing at the corner of the shop. He had evidently circled around, avoiding a direct approach, and moved in close from the upper end of the street.

"Howdy," he said in an uncertain voice. "Seen you come walking in. Who might you be?"

"It's him," the blacksmith said before Jud could reply. "Mark on this here horse is a J-Bar-J. That's what that rider said it'd be."

Hunter faced the two men coolly, the blacksmith to his left, the marshal on his right. Tom Ford had not quit, that was definite now. The rider mentioned had been his messenger sent on ahead to circulate a warning and, no doubt, make a promise of generous rewards. But it was no moment for irresolution.

"What's this all about?" he demanded bluntly.

130

The marshal's hand, resting on the butt of the pistol he wore, was trembling slightly and there was a nervous twitch to his lips.

"Ain't no sense asking that, Hunter. I got the word you was coming this way yesterday morning. They're wanting you for helping a woman murderer to escape and for stealing a horse—namely that there bay."

"Afraid you're some mixed up. Horse don't belong to me."

"Know that. You're riding a chestnut. You grabbed this here one for the woman to ride. Where is she?"

"Gone."

The lawman frowned, clawed at his chin. "Gone?" he echoed, and glanced at the blacksmith.

In that fraction of time Hunter drew his weapon, leveled it at the marshal. The elderly man's eyes flared with surprise and confusion.

"Aw, hell, Amos," the smithy said in a voice heavy with disgust. "Now you've gone and—"

"Never mind," Hunter cut in quietly as he stepped up and relieved the marshal of his pistol. "Just you get busy with that shoeing job."

Thrusting the old model Colt under his waistband, Jud motioned the lawman toward the rear of the shop.

"Long as you keep working," he said pointedly to the burly blacksmith, "your friend won't get hurt. Try something and he gets a bullet. That plain?"

The man shrugged, began to pump the bellows preparatory to fitting the bay's second shoe. Hunter, glancing about the interior of the shop, located what looked to be a storage room in the back. It would serve his purpose when the proper time came.

Pointing to a scarred rocking chair used probably by the smithy when work was slack, he said, "Sit down, Marshal. Everything'll be fine unless one or the other of you tries to be a hero."

The lawman seated himself grudgingly. "You ain't going to get far. I'm looking for that Ford fellow and his posse to show up tonight some-time."

"By then I'll be halfway to Prescott," Hunter replied with a fine but necessary disdain for the truth. "One thing you ought to know, this Tom Ford's all wrong."

"About what? Was his brother that got hisself killed and the woman was convicted by—"

"She wasn't the one who did it. I figure it could've been Ford himself, unloading the blame on her."

"That why you're helping her get away?"

Hunter nodded, waited until the blacksmith stopped clanging on his anvil. "Wasn't about to stand by and let them hang a woman for some-thing she wasn't guilty of."

132

"What if she'd been a man?"

"Expect I'd done the same thing."

The marshal stirred wearily. "Well, it ain't the way to go about something like that. If you thought she got a bad deal, then you should've gone to the law."

"Up where this all happened Tom Ford's the law. What he says, goes."

Again the lawman shifted. "Figured you'd feel that way," he said, and spat into the loose dust at his feet. "Always how it is. Man works hard, gets big, makes something of himself, then every jackleg comes along hates his guts and names him a sonofabitch."

"They're not always wrong," Hunter said drily, casting a side glance at the smithy. He was almost finished with the near hind leg. Best settle for only half a job, Jud decided. Waiting while the man put irons on the front hooves would be too risky. Other Burnt Pine residents might drop by the shop and he wanted no gunplay.

In silence he watched the blacksmith go about the final motions of his task, setting the shoe on squarely, driving home the nails to secure it and then rasping the edges of the hoof.

"I'm letting it go at that," he said as the man stepped back, started to wheel the bay around.

"Thought you wanted the whole job done?"

"Did, but I'm plain running out of time. . . . Move over there by the marshal."

The squat smithy, his smoked face dark, dropped the coarse file he still held into a workbox and crossed to the lawman's side.

"Now, both of you—inside the shed."

The marshal rose wordlessly and followed the blacksmith into the small storage area. At once Jud stepped up, swung the crude door shut, closed the hasp and dropped the pin into place. The old, rotting boards would not hold them long, he knew. The smithy had but to put his shoulder to the makeshift panel and rip it from its hinges.

Jud took the lawman's pistol from his waistband, laid it beside the rifle on the bench and turned to the bay.

"If you're smart," he said, glancing at the shed, "you'll stay right where you are for a spell because I'll be looking back. Could be I'm every bit as mean as Tom Ford claims I am," he added as he led the bay into the open and swung to the saddle.

17

It was not long until sundown, but they pushed on, regardless, Auralee on the chestnut, Hunter on the little bay since he was unwilling to take even the few moments necessary to exchange mounts when he rejoined her.

"That blacksmith'll mighty quick bust out of that closet," he explained after relating to her his experience in the settlement. "When he does he'll be turning loose a plenty mad marshal."

"Do you think they'll follow us?" Auralee wondered, looking back in the direction of the village.

"Maybe. Got my doubts, however. The marshal said something about Ford and his posse coming in. My guess is he'll wait for them."

Auralee sighed heavily. "I thought we had shaken him—had hoped so, anyway."

"Same here. Figured he'd given up back there before we crossed the Rio Grande. Guess I was selling him a mite short."

They rode on into the night until finally, for the sake of the horses, they were forced to halt. They made a dry camp in an arroyo, one deep enough to give them protection from the eyes of anyone searching the country for signs of a fire as well as from the cold, early morning wind that consistently sprang up an hour or so before dawn.

After a hasty breakfast they mounted and resumed the flight, Auralee again on the bay, his gait much improved by the new shoes he wore, Hunter once more astride the chestnut. They bore steadily toward the southwest all that day while a towering mass of dark mountains far to their right grew slowly larger and took on definite dimension.

Late in the afternoon during a brief stop to rest the horses, Auralee pointed toward them. "Are those the mountains we have to cross?"

"They're the Mogollons," he said. "It's the Peloncillos we're heading for." He looked off into the deep southwest. "Barely see them."

"It's taking so long," she murmured listlessly. "Seems like we've been riding for months."

Hunter grinned. "Not too far now—we're about halfway, maybe a little more. But we're doing good. Crossing these flats is easy on the horses and we're covering a lot of miles. If we hadn't lost time with the bay—"

"My fault," Auralee broke in bitterly. "I should have paid more attention."

"Wouldn't have made any difference. Shoe was worn out and he'd've lost it anyway. We'd still have had to hunt up a blacksmith."

She smiled at his efforts to dispel the blame she felt. Then, "What about the front hooves?"

"Plenty wore out, too," he admitted, "and

should've been replaced. But they're on solid. Had a look at them this morning."

"Will they last until we get to Nogales?"

"Probably, unless we run into bad luck. Have to take it careful when we get to the mountains, not let him loosen them in the rocks."

They mounted shortly after that, once more riding until well after dark before making camp.

"We're running low on water again," Auralee informed him as she set the pot of coffee over the fire.

He swore softly, realizing that in their haste to get away from Burnt Pine he'd neglected to refill the canteens.

"Have to make it last another day," he said. "Berrenda Creek's at the foot of those hills we were looking at just before dark. Be low this time of year, but it ought to have some water in it. We can be there by sundown tomorrow."

"Will the horses be able to stand it that long?"

"Have to. I'll treat them to a swallow in the morning before we leave. That and what they're getting from grazing will help."

Auralee glanced around at the scanty growth of thin, yellowed grass. "There's not much for them. It all looks dead."

"Be plenty of dew on it by morning and it's pretty good fodder no matter what you think. Cattle grow fat on it."

The next day was much like those that preceded

it, warm after the sun's arrival, and the wind had ceased. The country was little more than a vast, gracefully undulating plain rimmed by shadowy mountains. The sameness of it was monotonous and it seemed they were scarcely moving across its surface, but were in fact on a treadmill, since nothing appeared to change: the summer-faded growth, the rolling humps, the sandy arroyos, the grotesque cholla—all alike mile after mile under a sun that inched forward overhead in an unvarying, cloudless sky.

But they did come to its end—at the foot of a rambling chain of high hills which he told her were called the Mimbres—and the stream he had mentioned was there as promised, small and quite shallow but flowing, nevertheless.

They splurged in the rare comfort of a good camp where the horses found ample grazing as well as water, and despite the near-sundown coolness both Auralee and Hunter took advantage of the creek's proximity to bathe. She also seized the opportunity to again wash her dress, now dulled to a slate gray and showing the effects of continual hard wear.

Wrapped in their one blanket, she spread the garment over a framework of brush that he placed near the fire for her and stepped back, considered it fondly.

"I've always liked that dress. Emory did too. He bought it for me in New Orleans."

Hunter poured himself a second cup of coffee. High above in the last spears of sunlight that filled the heavens, a solitary vulture drifted in an ever widening circle.

"He mean a lot to you?"

Auralee was a long time in answering. "I suppose so," she said finally. "I'm not really sure I ever loved him."

Jud scratched at his jaw. The whiskery growth had gone unchecked for several days and was beginning to itch. He guessed he should warm up a little water in one of the tins, hone his skinning knife and scrape the beard off before turning in.

"Kind of a funny thing to say. You married him."

"I know, but I suppose it was sort of a whirlwind affair and I got caught up in it. He was the big handsome rancher with lots and lots of money, showering me with nice things and paying a lot of attention to me. When he asked me to marry him it was the natural thing to do."

Auralee paused, staring into the fire. "I guess I thought I loved him."

"Back in Kansas you found out different."

Auralee raised her head, looked at him squarely. "I'm not sure of that either because, well—I'm not certain I know what love really is."

A puzzled expression crossed Hunter's craggy features as he studied her. After a moment she again lowered her gaze to the fire.

"Can't hold me up as no expert, but seems to me that oughtn't to be hard to find out."

She turned to him at once, the quick motion setting small, golden lights dancing in her hair as the fire's reflection changed.

"Is that true? Should I know without even having to think about it?"

He shifted uneasily. "Like I said, you're talking to the wrong man about something like that. I figured you, or any woman'd, know for sure about such a thing."

"Then you don't understand what love is either?"

"Maybe not exactly. Always thought that liking to be with a woman, liking to hear her talk and laugh and the way she looks, and feeling tall when I'd hold her tight, would be love."

Auralee was staring at him intently. "No matter about anything else—having things like money, and a home, friends?"

"Don't see as they'd count."

She looked away again and resumed her sober contemplation of the flames. "All of your life," she said in a low voice, "you've just drifted along—alone. But I think you know more about what love is than anyone I've ever met."

Hunter scrubbed self-consciously at his beard. "Can't hardly believe that. Had my share of learning about just plain living and getting along with life, but what you're saying—" He broke off, at a loss for words with which to express himself.

Auralee nodded absently. "Maybe that's it. Maybe they're the same thing—loving and living—but it's only real and good when you're with the right person."

Jud picked up an empty tin and rose to his feet. "You're flying way over my head," he said, grinning, and started for the stream to get his shaving water. "Never was much of a hand to think on things like that. Was always sort of busy just living."

"That's what I mean," Auralee said. "It's feeling happy and contented with someone without needing others or anything."

He paused, squatting at the edge of the stream, and tried to understand what she was getting at. It was all too complicated for him, he decided, finally and unnecessary. He knew what he meant and the pivotal center of all such meaning was Auralee herself. Whatever else transpired in the universe was only incidental.

18

They began early and rode steadily that day, taking care to not press the horses unduly, only to keep them moving at a good pace broken by periodic rest halts.

During the forenoon, under a sky now banked along the horizon with rolling, cottony clouds, they skirted the irregular base of the Mimbres Mountains and then, as time and miles wore on, they found themselves once more on a great plain.

The remoteness into which Auralee had retreated on previous occasions had claimed her again and she spoke little during the stops, not at all while they were in the saddle. It was probable that a large measure of the quietude that gripped her stemmed from the knowledge that Tom Ford was still definitely in pursuit and that, upon reaching Burnt Pine, he would be given information that would undoubtedly spur him to greater effort.

As a result of her pensiveness, Jud once more fell to watching their back trail, troubling to look over his shoulder often, always taking advantage of the high places they crossed to lay a sharp and probing scrutiny upon the land.

But as the day aged he began to suspect that Ford was not on her mind as much as was something else. He tried gently to draw her out, thinking now that the fault might lie with him or that it was a matter in which he could be of help. His endeavor met with no success, however, eliciting only indifferent response, and so he gave it up.

A self-sufficient, often brooding man, inclined to silence himself, he understood and respected her need for solitude and making no further attempts to trespass, simply filled his hours with a satisfaction that came from having her nearby.

Late in the day a gray smudge hanging in the sky to the west drew their attention as they began to cast about for a suitable night camp.

"Lordsburg," he said. "Pretty fair town."

Auralee stared fixedly at the drifting haze scarring the blue. "A town," she murmured. "It would be nice to go there—get a room in a hotel, eat at a restaurant—"

He studied her quietly for a long minute. Then, "Can do it if you want, but it'll be risky. If Ford got word to a dump like Burnt Pine, he for sure passed it on to the law in a place big as Lordsburg. I'm willing, however, if it means a plenty to you."

"It doesn't," she said flatly. "I was only dreaming—maybe wishing. It would be foolish to take any chances now."

They resumed the trail, Auralee slipping again into her singular world of private thought while Jud continued his search of the empty land for a place to spend the night. A clump of cedars rose suddenly beyond a roll in the curving shoulder over which they were moving and offered possibilities. He slanted the chestnut toward it.

It proved to be an arroyo of some depth. They rode down into it, immediately dropping below the level of the surrounding country.

"Reckon we've had better camps," he said, dismounting, "but nobody'll spot us here."

Auralee only nodded, drew the bay to a halt and slipped from the saddle. She hadn't waited for him to lift her off, a small, ritualistic habit that had sprung up between them, and the oversight brought a frown to Hunter's face.

She caught it at once and shook her head. "I'm sorry—I wasn't thinking. I've been poor company today, I know. Getting tired, I guess."

"Can see how you would be. About the other, just want to be sure I didn't say something wrong—"

"It's nothing like that, Jud," she answered, and glanced around the couleelike cove in the wash. "This will make a fine camp. I'll start supper while you look after the horses." She started to walk away, halted abruptly. "How far are we from Nogales?"

He gave the distant mountains that rose in distinct and separate dark-shrouded masses ahead to their left and to their right a calculating consideration.

"Maybe five days," he said. "Could be less."

Auralee made no comment but moved on to prepare the meal, her features betraying neither dismay nor relief at the information. Hunter watched her for several moments, the disquiet within him heightened by her question, but after a bit he dismissed it all as weariness on her part plus an understandable anxiety to bring the long journey to an end, and went on about his customary duties of caring for the ever important horses.

Later, after the fire had died to embers and Auralee had sought out the comfort of their one blanket, he wandered off into the star-struck night, ostensibly to stretch his legs, but as soon as he was beyond earshot of the camp, he cut to his left and, climbing to the crest of a rise, threw his glance to the northeast. A grim smile pulled at the corners of his mouth.

Far in the distance the red eye of a campfire winked through the silvered darkness. Tom Ford and his posse; it could be no one else following so exact a course, one that overrode the very tracks the chestnut and the bay were leaving in their passage.

He remained there on the hill for a full hour while the muted sounds of the night hung around him—the rustling of small animals in quest of food, the feathery swish of an owl, the bark of coyotes challenging from the faraway slopes.

He and Auralee still had a good lead on Ford and they were in a position to hold it. Unless some unexpected delay developed, they could reach the Mexican border at least a half-day ahead of him—and that was all that was necessary. But he'd not tell Auralee about it, Jud decided as he headed back for camp. To know Ford was that near would only increase her worry.

He did, however, take the precaution of getting an early start. Ford, impatient now that by a stroke of good fortune found himself drawing close, would be up and riding also—and on unquestionably stronger horses. It was possible that he had even exchanged for fresh mounts in the settlement; if so, he could be expected to make every effort toward ending the chase. The rancher would be fully aware of the difficulties he would face with Mexican authorities once the border lay between him and his quarry and he sought to lead an armed party across it. Thus he would do everything possible to end the pursuit short of the line.

Hunter pushed the horses hard until mid-afternoon, when they found themselves riding due south in a broad green valley that he called the San Simeon. Mountains were now to either side of them, and Auralee, eyes on the formation to their right, repeated the question she had asked days before.

"Are those the mountains we have to cross?"

He considered the massive eruption of yellowish rocks, rugged bluffs and timberless slopes and nodded. "They're the Peloncillos, all right, only we'll do our crossing farther down. Better trail and it brings us out below the Chiricahuas."

"More mountains?"

He grinned at her expression of dismay. "On the Arizona side. Won't have to climb over them. Once we're on the yonder slopes of this pile, it's a straight run into Mexico."

Jud thought that would cheer her, but she accepted it with only a faint movement of her head. It was almost as if, their goal now in sight, she was regretting the achievement. He shrugged, mystified by her—mystified as he'd always been by the few women he had become acquainted with in his lifetime.

They reached the trail just at dark. He did not call an immediate halt, however, but continued a distance up the grade to a deep ravine where they could be well hidden during the night. It wasn't a comfortable location, the walls of the wash being close by, steep and difficult to enter from the trail, and too small for the horses, necessitating their being picketed in a separate area several yards removed.

Auralee voiced no complaint, but he knew she wondered about his choice.

"This is Indian country," he explained in a low

147

voice. "Need to go quiet and keep out of sight as much as we can from now on."

She stiffened slowly as fear overtook her. Stepping quickly to her side, he put his arms about her. "We'll be all right long as we're careful."

Auralee clung to him for a time and then, pulling away, looked up toward the higher levels of the slopes. The last of the sun's glare was almost gone, turning the ragged contours dark and foreboding.

"Do they live here—have a village, I mean?"

"No. Their camps—these Apaches don't have villages—are closer to the Chiricahuas. Only hunting parties ever come this far."

Unnoticed, he looked beyond her to the valley below. There was no campfire visible. Either Ford and the posse had not yet halted for the night or else they too were taking no chances with the Apaches.

"Best we do no cooking," he said. "Have to get by on hardtack and canned stuff—tomatoes, maybe, and some of that jerky. This time tomorrow we'll be in Mexico. Can fix up a good meal then."

Auralee nodded to show her understanding and, taking the flour sack, rummaged about for suitable articles. They ate in silence and retired early without the friendly, warming benefit of a campfire. Later, during the long, uncomfortable hours, Hunter roused and had his look into the San Simeon. There was still no indication of Ford.

Well before dawn, driven to wakefulness by the biting cold, they rose. Breakfasting on the biscuits and dried meat salved by water from their canteens, they shortly crossed to where the horses waited and prepared to move out. Their mounts ready, Hunter boosted Auralee onto her saddle and turned to the chestnut.

He froze, the distinct thud of a horse's hoof coming to them in the clear, crisp air. Placing a finger to his lips for silence, he lifted her off the bay. Motioning for her to remain, he bent low and worked his way a short distance up the wash to where he could see the trail.

In only moments he returned, his face drawn to taut lines. Taking her by the shoulders he looked at her intently.

"Don't make a sound," he whispered. "We've got visitors—Apaches."

Hunter felt the girl start in his grasp, watched her stifle the cry that leaped to her lips, and drew her close. . . . He hadn't told her the worst: that they could not move back down the slope; Tom Ford and his posse were there. They were trapped in between.

19

"Are they coming this way?"

Auralee was trembling against him and her voice was so low Jud could scarcely hear her words. He shook his head.

"Camped above us. Been there all night, I expect. Can see about a half a dozen of them."

"Then they were there when we came in—"

"Maybe. Plenty glad we were quiet and didn't build a fire."

The trembling had ceased and she seemed to have regained control of herself. Glancing over her shoulder, she said, "Can't we slip back through the brush?"

It was senseless to keep it from her any longer. "No chance. Ford and the posse are down there."

A fresh gust of fear swept her. She caught at his arm, looked up into his set features.

"When?"

"Spotted them a couple of nights ago—back on the flat. Probably camped somewhere close to the foot of the slope right now if they haven't already started up the trail."

"Then we're caught in the middle?"

"What it amounts to, but don't give up yet. Those Apaches could be headed the other way."

A low sob escaped her throat. "Oh, Jud, what can we do?"

"Wait it out," he replied. "One thing sure, we've got to get farther away from the trail." He paused, studied her closely. "Means we'll have to move quiet—quieter than you ever figured you could do. Think you can do that?"

Auralee nodded.

"We'll swing across, work our way up the slope. Saw a rock ledge that'll be a good place to hide behind."

"What about the horses?"

"They'll have to stay where they are. Make too much racket if we take them. Just hoping they don't get restless."

Crouching low, he took her by the hand and started across the ravine, taking each step with elaborate care, watchful for scraping brush and loose rock that could set up a noise and draw the Apaches' attention.

It required a long, tedious ten minutes to climb out of the wash, pass below the still-dozing horses, luckily trail-worn and caring little about what occurred around them, and reach the ledge. The jutting mass fell short of expectations; there was hardly any depression back of the shell, which faced the trail, where he had planned for them to lie low. But it would have to suffice. He dared not press their luck by searching for a better place.

He could see the Indians, however, and that was important. Motioning Auralee to sit at the base of the rocks, he drew himself to the level of the fronting terrain and, peering through a clump of snakeweed, considered them.

His hasty count had been correct; there were six of them sprawled and squatting about in a small clearing. Evidently they had been there all night, or most of it, and the miracle of how Auralee and he had approached so near them without being seen or heard again struck him.

As if in answer to the puzzle, one of the dark-haired men, sitting with his back to a stump, leaned forward and, picking up a bottle, tipped it to his lips. It was empty. He uttered a quick guttural word and hurled the container off into the brush. Somewhere along the way they had gotten liquor, probably having ambushed a luckless traveler, and spent the night in drunkenness.

The remaining braves stirred. One rose to his feet and walked to the edge of the open ground, scratching himself vigorously as he moved. Halting, he looked off into the brush. Jud followed his gaze, saw a blur of color in the brush. The man was checking on their horses. After a time the Apache returned to his companions, said something in his native tongue. The braves drew themselves sluggishly upright.

They were preparing to ride. Hunter eased himself back into the shallow pocket behind the ledge and hunched beside Auralee. She faced him, fear showing in her eyes.

"Are they coming?"

Drawing his pistol, he shook his head. "Getting ready to leave. Don't know which way they'll be going yet."

Hunter drew back the hammer to release the weapon's cylinder and turned the circular magazine until the empty chamber was at the loading gate. Thumbing a cartridge from his belt, he filled the chamber and then reset the heavy gun, now completely loaded. *Six shots—six Apaches,* he thought grimly. This was one time he couldn't afford to miss. Each bullet must find its target for the simple reason he'd never get the opportunity to reload.

Staying behind the snakeweed, he raised his head again for a look. Two of the braves were on their horses, the remaining four still standing in the center of the clearing. A discussion of some sort was taking place, apparently an exchange of ideas on where they should go or, perhaps, what they should do.

The sun, out now and at full strength, was reaching into the ragged growth on the slope, ferreting out the shadows and making all things clear. Hunter could see the trail, a dozen strides this side of the Apaches; they too had taken the precaution of drawing off the beaten course a practical distance, either hopeful of waylaying other pilgrims or as a matter of personal safety.

They were somewhat less than a hundred yards away through the screen of intervening brush, and Jud could see them clearly. The sun was striking against their copper-colored bodies, glinting off their coarse black hair, highlighting the planes of their broad, strong faces as they conversed in the quick, explosive manner of their kind.

He felt Auralee's hand upon his leg and looked down. The strain of waiting, the brutal tension of the dragging moments, were having their effect upon her. Taut lines pulled at her mouth and near-terror now shone in her eyes. Lowering himself to her side, Jud took her trembling hand in his.

"Still there. Can't seem to make up their minds what they want to do," he said before she could speak. He hefted the pistol. "Don't worry. This evens the odds."

"But—there are six of them, you said—"

"And six bullets in this gun. One apiece."

Giving her a reassuring grin, he raised himself again. The last Apache was mounting, settling his lithe body on a small spotted horse. In single file they began to move out. Hunter's muscles tensed. They were heading downslope. If they stayed on or near the trail all would go well—

assuming the bay or the chestnut didn't attract attention by stamping or making some other noticeable sound.

He frowned. The braves, now outside the open ground where they had spent the night, were separating, spreading into a forage line as if beginning a hunting expedition and hoping to flush before them whatever game it was they sought.

Jud allowed himself to sink slowly. One of the Apaches was moving directly toward him. Apparently he intended to work his way across the slope to the ledge and there begin his abreast descent. Avoiding Auralee's eyes, Jud tried to figure a way to meet the approaching threat. That the Indian would not see them crouched behind the rocks was impossible.

And if by some stroke of good fortune he did not, they would be no better off. Within only moments he would encounter the horses, both saddled and ready to ride, realize instantly their owners were close by, and set up a cry for the rest of the party. . . . If only there were some means for getting at the brave, silencing him and preventing his giving an alarm.

Again Hunter raised up behind the stiff ball of snakeweed. The Apache was still coming, a hunched, gleaming shape on a black pony less than a dozen yards away. Abruptly one of the Indians farther over barked a warning. The brave halted instantly, twisted about and looked toward the speaker. More blunt-edged words broke the hush.

The brave dropped from his horse hurriedly, face now turned downslope toward the valley. He called softly to the others and then, hunched low, began to move silently forward through the brush, rifle poised in his hands. Inching to one side, Hunter located three more of the Apaches. They too had dismounted and like drifting shadows were also headed downgrade.

The posse . . .

It dawned upon Jud suddenly. The Indians had spotted Ford and his men either nearby in the valley or, more likely, at the foot of the mountain and starting up the trail, and were laying an ambush. He gave that thought. It didn't help much. The brave nearest them would still pass close to the ledge. Now, however, he was off his horse and the chances of silencing him without alerting the others were somewhat better.

Jud settled back to Auralee's side. Not mentioning Tom Ford, he said, "They're off their horses. Got one coming this way. Aim to try and shut him up before he can yell for the others."

She nodded, the knuckles of her tightly locked fingers showing white.

"Main thing is keep quiet—no matter what happens. If I don't make it, crawl off into the brush and hide. Rest of them will come fast. Wait until they've had their look around and gone on, then head off up the mountain."

There were tears in her eyes, from fear or because the thought of something dire might befall him filled her with grief, he had no way of knowing. Her voice was only a faint, faltering whisper.

"Where can I go?"

"Cross the mountain, head south. Long walk, but you can make it—and you might find yourself a horse. There's a town on the border they call Douglas. You'll be all right once you get there."

Auralee shook her head, a resoluteness coming into her manner. "I won't even try—not without you."

Hunter grinned. "Not planning on you having to. Just wanted you to know—in case."

Shifting the pistol to his right hand, he once more drew himself up behind the snakeweed. The brave was almost upon them.

20

Motionless, scarcely breathing, Hunter watched the Apache draw closer. A young brave, his high-boned features were set, his black agate eyes partly closed while the muscles of his lithe body shifted smoothly beneath their gleaming copper cover as he slunk through the brush. He would pass the edge of the rock shelf no more than an arm's length away.

Jud, coolly calculative, knew he must strike swiftly and accurately. If he could manage to drag the Apache down below the rocks, the necessary commotion would less likely be noticed by the other Indians since they would be cut off from view. But there was a risk; the struggle would then take place directly in front of Auralee, only inches from her, in fact, and considering her state of mind he was not sure she could weather what undoubtedly would be a bloody fight to the death, without screaming. That she was near the breaking point was only too evident.

Clearing his mind, he concentrated his capacities on the brave and the task at hand. He couldn't afford to plan, only to take things as they came.

The Apache was almost to the ledge, body hunched, gaze locked on something farther down the slope. The posse, probably. Apparently he and the others were hurrying to reach a lower position where the ambush could be more effective. Had he chosen a route half a dozen strides more to the south he would have moved by unnoticing.

One of the horses stirred. The brave froze, his dark set features turned toward the south. With his broad back to the ledge the ideal moment for attack was at hand, but Hunter waited; the Apache was near, but it would be necessary to climb up and over the rocks to get to him. Better to hold off until he had dropped to a lower point where they would both be on the same level.

The brave remained poised, seemingly not certain of what he had heard—if anything. The moments dragged by. The crouched figure continued to hang motionless as his body, naked from the waist up, began to glisten brighter as the sun's steadily rising heat laid a sweat shine upon it. Abruptly he straightened, swung his attention again to the foot of the slope and moved on.

He drew abreast the ledge, was a step beyond. Hunter, gripping his pistol by the barrel, pivoted slowly with him and gathered his muscles. Suddenly he came upright, threw himself at the Apache.

The brave heard the faint crunch of gravel and wheeled. Jud met him head on, weapon swinging. The Apache jerked to one side, took the shocking blow on his shoulder, tried to pull away. Hunter's fingers locked onto his coarse hair, checked him.

The Indian grunted, heaved forward, striving to break free. Hunter, his hope of silencing the man quickly now lost, threw his arm about the rank, sweaty body, hauled backward and dragged the brave down into the shallow sink behind the rocks.

They fell hard. The Apache, partly on top, dropped his rifle. A knife glittered in his hand. Jud, still clinging to the man's hair, yanked savagely at the greasy mass, struck again with the pistol. The butt caught the brave above the left eye. Stunned, he rocked to one side. Hunter released his grip on the man's hair, rolled clear and came to his feet.

He lunged at the Apache, vaguely aware that Auralee had not uttered a sound, that she had drawn herself back against the ledge, had seized a rock and was striking at the brave with it.

The momentum of his charge drove the Apache, rising to meet him, against the ledge. The knife fell from his hand as his head smashed into the wall of granite. Heaving for breath, soaked with sweat, Hunter pulled himself upright as the brave sank slowly. From nearby Auralee watched the limp body settle with a dazed sort of fascination.

Moving to the edge of the rocks quickly, Jud listened. The noise of the fight could not possibly have gone unnoticed. Almost at once a guttural word reached him. The brave's nearest companion had heard and was voicing his wonder. Hunter rode out a long minute. The questioning word came again, this time louder and more insistent.

Desperate, Jud cupped his hands to his mouth and grunted, imitating the tones of the Apaches back in the clearing where he had first observed them. Then tense, pistol ready, he waited. If the ruse failed, the suspicious brave would soon appear.

Time lagged. Over in the near distance he heard the dry rattle of displaced gravel, audible only briefly. Again there was silence. One of the Indians' horses shifted and up on the mountain a dove cooed. Relief slipped through him. Well down the slope he saw movement. A dark hunched figure slipped quickly into a patch of oak brush, disappeared. Jud's reply had satisfied the Indian.

He spun to Auralee. She had regained her composure and was watching him closely.

"They've gone. Got to get out of here—fast."

She crossed to him hurriedly, pointing at the sprawled brave. "What about him? Won't he come to?"

"Not for a few minutes and then it won't matter," he replied, and extended his hand to her.

"Keep low," he warned her, and with the girl at his heels, started down the grade toward the arroyo where the horses waited. They reached the wash, freed the animals and led them into the open.

Hunter raised a hand to halt Auralee while he studied the grade below. The Apaches could still be on the move, or they might have reached the point where they planned to hide. There was no way of knowing which since the brush closed off all view of them. The same held true of Tom Ford and the posse. That they were down there somewhere was certain, but their exact whereabouts was a mystery.

"Save time if we'd cross over, get on the trail," Jud said.

"Won't they—somebody see us?"

"That's what's bothering me—but I reckon it won't matter now."

He moved off at once, leading the chestnut, picking a route through the brush and rocks. The noise of the horses' passage seemed loud to him, but there was nothing to be done about it except hurry and keep a sharp watch below for any signs that the Apaches had heard and were doubling back to investigate.

He came to the trail, halted, turned to help Auralee, but she was already going onto her saddle. He mounted at once and, motioning for her to pull out in front of him, started the climb.

Immediately Auralee stopped the bay, a small cry bursting from her lips. Drawing his pistol,

Jud spurred up to her, looked ahead. Sighing, he holstered his weapon. The Apaches had left their horses in the brush nearby; Auralee had mistaken them for more Indians.

"Keep moving," he said. "Sooner we're off this side of the mountain, the better I'll like it. Going to be a regular war cut loose down there pretty quick."

21

They had reached the top of the long slope and were dropping off onto its opposite side when the first quick spatter of gunshots came to them. Hunter did not slacken the pace but pushed on, holding the horses to a steady trot on the fairly steep grade.

The hollow-sounding reports dwindled, stopped entirely for the space of several minutes, and then broke out again, this time continuing without a letup. The first blasts had been the ambush, the surprise attack of the Apaches, Hunter guessed. Then followed the quiet period while Ford and his men recovered and got themselves set. The subsequent shooting was the counterattack when the rancher and his posse—whatever was left of it—moved in to drive the braves from hiding and kill them. Tom Ford would brook little delay and stand even less interference; he had already demonstrated that.

Midway down the slope, Hunter caught sight of movement on the trail far below them. Swinging in beside Auralee, he crowded the bay off into the brush.

"Another bunch of Apaches," he said, and pulled out in front of her.

It was a larger party—ten, possibly fifteen. He

could not be sure. They had halted, apparently also having heard the gunshots. For a time they did not move, simply sat their ponies while Hunter and Auralee watched from the shelter of a cedar clump, and then, when the firing died off, the Indians resumed their course northward along the base of the mountain.

"Headed away from us," Jud said, motioning Auralee back onto the trail.

The fact that no more shooting could be heard indicated that the fight was over, that Ford and his men, assuming they had survived the ambush, would be taking to the trail again, and the lead Auralee and Hunter had built up had shrunk even more. There was no time to waste.

They rode on, reached the bottom of the grade and swung hard left, pointing into another land of broad plains bordered with mountains. The sun was high now and the feel of its heat was distinct on this west side of the Peloncillos and soon began to have its effect upon the horses. But Hunter refused to slow their gait.

"Got to keep going," he said to Auralee's suggestion they halt and rest the mounts. "Can't be sure how close Ford is."

They were out in the open, on a broad flat broken here and there with outcroppings of black lava rock. Gaunt cactus, needle-tipped yucca and the ever present snakeweed studded the reddish earth where there was none of the

165

grayish grass that blanketed the country. In the arroyos mesquite and an occasional paloverde tree disrupted the similarity.

Finally, well out in the center of the limitless land, they were compelled to halt. The bay, covered with lather, was beginning to show signs of caving in. The chestnut was only a little better. Jud, spotting a fairly wide stand of creosote bush spurring out from a dark wall of lava, angled toward it.

"Can spare one hour," he said, coming off the saddle. "When that's gone, we move."

Auralee, studying his set features as he lifted her from the heaving bay, frowned. "But in only an hour can they—"

"Ford's not far behind us," he cut in, pointing to the sloping end of a line of bluish mountains in the south, "and that's Mexico. We're too close now to let anything stop us."

Her expression of concern altered at once and she became sober, filled with that remoteness he had encountered earlier.

"Mexico," she murmured. "When?"

"By dark. Sooner if the horses stand up." He turned, looked back over the stark, savage land they had crossed. "Posse's not in sight—but they'll be coming."

His estimation of Tom Ford's tenacity now equaled that of Auralee's. She shrugged, almost hopefully.

"Maybe not. Those Apaches—they could have stopped him."

"Doubt it. More in Ford's bunch and they were better-armed. Indians were sure to get the worst of it."

She strolled to the edge of the arroyo and began to finger the yellow blossoms of a clump of desert marigold. From a precarious perch on a round-topped rock nearby a lizard watched with beady eyes.

"Are we safe from Indians here?"

"Prob'ly. Apaches keep pretty close to the hills, and the soldiers patrol through here sort of regularly."

"Then it's only Tom we need to worry about."

"Him and the horses," Hunter replied, and crossed the arroyo to a slight rise where he could continue to watch for the rancher and his posse.

The far-reaching flat was empty, but there was no real assurance in that; Ford could be intentionally keeping his men in the deep washes and thereby staying out of sight. He guessed it all depended on how Ford figured it—whether it was better to ride the level ground at a speed that took heavy toll of the horses, or travel in the arroyos at a slower pace and hope, by remaining unseen, to close the gap unsuspectedly.

After a time Hunter returned to the wash. Auralee had seated herself on the wall of the embankment, taking shade from one of the larger bushes. She did not look up as he approached and he saw that she had again withdrawn into that deep shell of silence.

"Have to get moving," he said, taking up the reins of the horses and leading them to her. "Next stop's Mexico."

Wordless, she allowed him to boost her onto the saddle, waiting while he swung aboard the chestnut, and had his searching look to the north, and then followed him up and out onto the more solid ground of the plain.

Hunter set a direct course for a low, triangular peak on the horizon. Using it as a marker for crossing the border would allow them to enter at a safe distance from the settlement that lay in the area. Likely they would have no difficulties in crossing over unseen, but he was cautious and realized it was unwise to underestimate Tom Ford. The less conspicuous Auralee and he could make themselves, the better.

They progressed at a slower pace than earlier, but it was one that steadily consumed the miles of empty land. Near sundown they spotted a group of riders far to the west. They were moving away from them, however, and were no cause for alarm. Probably pilgrims on their way to Bisbee, Jud told Auralee. He'd heard the mining town was booming, that jobs were plentiful; a man would have no trouble finding work there.

Once more herself, Auralee considered his words gravely, reading the thoughts that he had left unspoken.

"You could never be a miner, Jud, you know that. It's not your kind of life."

His thick shoulders stirred. "Could be I'd not find it so bad. We could hunt us up a house, start a home."

"You'd die—doing that kind of work. I'd never let you do it."

He gave her a direct, level glance. "Be worth it to me."

"To me too—you and a home and all—but there must be better jobs around."

"Sure haven't come across one in quite a spell. Anyway, you can't always have it just the way you want. Sometimes you have to settle for less—and there'll be a price tag on that too."

"I know," she murmured.

He glanced to the west. The sun was below the ragged skyline and hurling its final lances of flaming color into the blue.

"Going to hit it about right. Want to do our crossing after dark."

"Why? Are we apt to have trouble?"

"Mexicans are a bit touchy about folks just riding in. Like to know who you are and what's bringing you there. I figure if they don't catch us, then we won't have to answer any questions—and if we don't answer any questions, they won't be able to tell Tom Ford anything when he shows up."

Auralee stiffened. "I thought we'd be safe from him once we were in Mexico!"

"Should be unless he manages somehow to sneak that young army he's got with him across—and even if he does, he'll find it hard to keep from being seen by the *Federales*—the Mexican soldiers. They don't take kindly to armed bands of *Americanos* just moving in, doing what they please. . . . Expect we'll be safe enough."

They pressed on as the night settled over the land. Lights began to blink in the distance, and far off in the southwest a rifle shot sounded, the echo flat and wavering as it floated through the hush. Later they heard the drumming of fast-running horses moving east, but they could see nothing because of the rolling contour of the country and the gathering clouds that had piled up to mask the moon.

Finally, in a deep gash in the brush-studded flat lying well below the triangular peak, Jud Hunter drew the chestnut to a halt and turned to Auralee.

"Reckon we're here," he said in an easy, satisfied voice as he dismounted. "This is Mexico."

The expression of happiness and relief he expected to see on her features was missing as he lifted her down. Instead he saw only that unfathomable remoteness that so baffled and disturbed him. Frowning, he started to step back, but she clung to him, face buried against his chest. After a few moments she looked up at him.

"Jud, let's not go to Nogales—let's just keep going."

22

Hunter stared at the girl incredulously. "Not go? Hell, that's the reason we—"

"I know, but I've changed my mind. I want to forget Nogales, find some place where we can live—"

He stilled her with a shake of his head. "Can't think of anything I'd not let you do or would do for you myself, except that. We've got to go there, find those friends of yours and get your name cleared."

"That doesn't matter. Let them think what they will."

"Not that easy. Ford and the law will be hunting you the rest of your life—and that's worse than being dead. Know firsthand because I walked in that pair of boots myself once for killing a man."

"You killed a—"

"Wasn't me that did it, but I caught the blame. Didn't like the idea of hanging for somebody else's doings, so I got away. Dodged the law for better'n a year and that was pure hell. Was always wondering if some marshal or some bounty hunter was on my trail, or waiting around the next bend in the road, or maybe just setting back in some town looking for me to show up.

"Got so jumpy I couldn't live with myself or

172

get along with anybody else, so one day I walked into a sheriff's office and turned myself in. Was a right pleasant surprise to find out I wasn't wanted no more. Man who'd done the killing had owned up to it and cleared me."

Hunter tightened his arms about the girl. "Not going to let you go through what I did that year. Does something to your insides, makes you see things all wrong, and I don't want you changed from what you are now. . . . We'll ride on to Nogales, get you squared away. Then we can go anywhere you want, anytime we please, and it'll be nobody's business but our own."

Head down, Auralee turned from him. Taking the flour sack of food, again growing light, she set about preparing a late meal while he turned to the customary chore of caring for the horses.

They moved out early that next morning for Nogales, now something less than three days' ride to the west, keeping well back from the border and on the alert for soldiers, who regularly patrolled the area. Twice they saw mounted groups of the brightly uniformed men, but on both occasions they were able to get out of sight quickly and go unnoticed.

The second day, hot and dusty, passed without incident, but on the morning of the third, riders appeared in the distance, following, as they were, a course below the line. They were a good two miles off and Hunter could make no recognition, but within him, as the hours passed and the horsemen continued to come on, seemingly dogging their very trail, a conviction began to solidify.

He said nothing to Auralee of his belief, but eventually she took note of the party and, swinging the bay in beside him, pointed excitedly at the riders.

"That's Tom Ford—I know it is!"

"Maybe," Hunter replied. "Guess he could've slipped across the border same as we did or he might've had some legal papers that let him do it. Good chance it's somebody else, too. Lot of folks probably do their trading in Nogales."

"How much farther is it?" she asked, looking ahead anxiously.

"Smoke you see, that's it. About two hours, I'd say."

Again she glanced at the riders. "They're closer."

Hunter was aware of that. He could make out six members in the party, one of which was riding a white horse. There had been eight in the posse at the start; two had probably been lost in the Apache ambush. They were coming on at a gallop despite the heat.

"Reckon that's Ford all right," Hunter said, a note of grimness coming into his tone. "But we can still beat him to Nogales."

"What good will it do now?" Auralee said in

a lost voice. "He's crossed over—following us again."

"Something we'll face up to later," he answered. "Let's get moving."

Jud spurred the chestnut into a lope and, with the bay quickly falling in beside him, led the way across the sunbaked ground, through sandy arroyos and down narrow ravines at a hard gait. Ahead houses began to appear, mere dots at first but gradually taking shape as the laboring horses pounded on. Behind them the six riders held their place, neither gaining nor losing.

Jud and Auralee drew near, came abreast of and passed a man and a woman in loose cotton clothing and straw hats, each riding an undersized gray burro on the way to the settlement. Their presence reminded Hunter of the ever possible danger from the *Federales* and the very real probability of encountering a patrol when they drew near the town.

Perhaps such would work to their advantage. If the officer in charge of the soldiers could be made to understand their predicament and grant them protection from Tom Ford until Auralee could reach her friends—

He shook off the idea. It would be difficult to explain. He spoke only a few words of Spanish and Mexican *Federales* were notorious for their aversion to *Americanos* who crossed the border to evade the law. Once caught, along with Ford

175

and his posse, who surely would be taken in also, the most they could hope for was to be escorted to the American side of the border and set free.

Only Auralee would not be free. Ford would have her, and with or without the sanction of the local authorities, he'd take her back to Kansas and the gallows that awaited—awaited both of them, Jud figured—if the rancher had his way.

He glanced at her. She was hunched forward on her saddle, features set, the profile of her face soft-edged even in the harsh sunlight. Small patches of moisture shone on her cheeks and there was desperation in the firm line of her lips.

"Not far," he called, pointing to the scatter of houses looming ahead.

She nodded, managed a smile. The bay was beginning to break and he gave thought to the possibility that the horse would go down. If so, Jud would scoop Auralee up behind him on the chestnut, which, though tired, was still holding up well.

Turning, he looked back at the posse. Ford was in the center of the pack and slightly ahead. They had put on a burst of speed and were now less than a mile away. But Nogales was at hand.

"Your friends—where do they live?" he yelled, making himself heard above the pounding hooves of the horses.

"Not sure exactly. The letter said in a house at the south end of town."

Hunter swore. "Takes in quite a few."

"It'll be right on the edge—a mud brick like the others, but it'll have a wire fence around it and a big tree shading it."

That narrowed it considerably. Fence was an expensive item and few native residents would be able to afford it. . . . The south edge . . .

The first houses were before them. Hunter began to veer the horses left. It would be better to circle the town, not attempt to cut through it at such a fast pace, for there would be people moving about on the streets. Besides, there were the *Federales* to think of.

They reached the last of the squat adobe structures in the line that faced them, rounded the corner and bore straight on.

"There it is!" Auralee cried, pointing to a house much like all others except for the stretched netting that surrounded it.

Hunter slowed the gelding. "Keep going, I'm waiting here for Ford."

She whirled to him. "No—they'll kill you!"

"Maybe not. Main thing is for you to get to your friends. I'll meet you there later."

He glanced over his shoulder. The posse was not to be seen, briefly blocked from view by intervening houses, but the rancher would have noted the course they had taken.

"Go on! Best Ford don't know which place you went into."

"No!" Auralee said again. There was a softness in her eyes, but her chin jutted forward stubbornly. "I won't let you face them alone, Jud. Either you come with me or I'll stay, too."

Hunter threw an anxious look behind him. The posse was just swinging into sight. "All right!" he shouted, and spurred up beside her.

23

They pounded down the dusty lane toward the fenced house. They wheeled into the yard through the open gate and Auralee drew the bay to a heaving, panting stop.

"The back—go around to the back!" Jud shouted.

It would be better. Tom Ford was still too far away to see exactly which structure they would be entering. But Jud's caution to Auralee was too late. The girl was already off her saddle, running toward the door.

"Jack—Jack!" she was yelling.

Hunter left the chestnut, hit the ground solidly on his heels. Slapping both horses on the rump and sending them trotting for the rear of the place in the faint hope that Ford was yet unaware of their exact destination, he turned to follow Auralee. A hard grin pulled at the corners of his mouth. The precaution would go for nothing; in the adjoining yard a man was squatting in the shadow of a wall and was watching him with puzzled interest. Tom Ford had but to ask him.

The door of the house was open. Jud hurried through it into a sparsely furnished room, halted as it slammed shut behind him. Wheeling, he faced a tall, handsome man dressed in a gray suit who was studying him curiously. Auralee, close to the window and peering out, turned. She made a small gesture.

"He's the friend I told you about, Jud," she said heavily. "Jack Conger."

Hunter accepted the hand extended to him. Its skin was soft, white, the fingers long and tapering—a gambler. "Friend? I thought you said friends."

"I did," she murmured, looking down. "It was a lie."

Conger frowned. "A lie? And what's all the hurry? Something go wrong?"

Auralee nodded. "Tom Ford. He trailed us all the way. He's out there now—looking for us."

Conger's face darkened angrily. "You let him follow you here?"

"Couldn't help it. We—Jud—tried everything, but he just kept on coming, even across the border."

Hunter, eyes narrowed, listened in silence. Outside he heard the thud of horses racing by— Ford still in pursuit. He'd quickly see that he'd lost them and would double back, asking questions of anyone he encountered. The man in the adjoining yard would supply the answers.

"You get the money?"

At Conger's question Jud swung his attention sharply to Auralee. She was nodding woodenly.

"Twenty thousand. That's all I could manage,"

she said, fingering the slight fold beneath the waistband of her petticoat. The pocketed strip of cloth she had made to carry money was exactly in place. "They put me in jail before I could get more."

"Jail? What for?"

"They think it was me that shot Emory—were going to hang me for it. They would have if Jud hadn't helped me get away."

"Wondered what was taking you so long," the gambler said. He crossed to the window, glanced out, spun about. "Got to get out of here. Can use the back way. Where's the money?"

"Safe," Auralee said, eyes on the floor.

"Give it to me—"

She ignored him, lifting her glance to Hunter. "I'm sorry, Jud. Sorry for everything. This is why I didn't want to come here."

Conger's arm reached out. His lean fingers wrapped themselves about her arm, closed. Auralee winced.

"So that's how it is!" he snapped. "Well, it's a damn good thing you didn't try crossing me. The money—hand it over!"

Hunter, anger tearing at him for many reasons as understanding began to take shape in his mind, stepped forward. His knotted fist came down hard on the gambler's wrist, breaking his tight grip.

"Let her be!"

Conger, features again coloring, stepped back. He stared at Hunter for a long moment through small glittering eyes, and then a sneer curled his lips.

"I see what this's all about," he said in a mocking tone. "I thought you'd just been hired to do a job, but no, she's hooked you too, same as she does every other man she gets around. Mister, you've been played for a rube, a sucker—another easy mark she euchered into doing a favor for her. She's my woman. Belongs one hundred percent to me—Jack Conger."

Auralee had turned from them and was facing the wall as she removed the jacket Jud had lent her. Hunter considered her slight figure coldly.

"That true?"

She nodded woodenly, began to do something with the front of her dress.

"All that talking we did about us—"

"Forget it, cowboy!" Conger broke in. "We're through with you, and knowing Auralee like I do, I expect you got well paid for your services. What's more, we're not in the market for a partner. The twenty thousand I'm getting for shooting that rancher she took on as a husband is not enough to spread your way."

"You killed Ford?" Jud asked in a low, barely controlled voice.

Jack Conger smiled, nodded. "Sure. Whole thing was a little scheme of mine. I let Auralee marry the sucker when he went mooncalfing after her in New Orleans. Found out first he had plenty of money, of course.

"Rode up to Kansas after they'd got themselves settled and she'd had time to get her hooks into his cashbox. Then I put a bullet in him and came here to wait for her. Didn't expect them to throw her in jail for it, however. Thought they'd blame some bum. . . . Now, that set things straight in your mind?"

Jud Hunter was trembling, racked with furious hatred for Conger and for the way the man had used Auralee. Likely it hadn't been the first time—but it sure as hell was the last.

"It's straight," he said coldly. "If you've got a gun on you, draw it because I'm going to—"

"You—Auralee!"

It was Tom Ford's voice, cutting suddenly into Hunter's words.

"Know you're in there, and you're not getting away. Got the place surrounded. I'm giving you one minute to come out!"

At Ford's harsh demand Auralee stiffened. He had caught up with them just as she'd always known, down deep, that he would. Now it was too late—too late for her, for Jack and most important of all, for Jud Hunter. But maybe there was a chance for him. Tom would have little against him, only that he'd helped her to escape. With her accounted for, maybe he'd forget about Jud.

She looked down at the cotton money belt folded into a square in her hands. Opening the pocket of the jacket she had been wearing, she stuffed the money inside and buttoned the flap. If he managed to get away he would at least have that, although it could be weeks, perhaps months, before he discovered it.

She hoped he'd not be foolish and stiff-necked and refuse to keep it. After all, it was her money. She had been Emory Ford's lawful wife and it became hers after his death—no matter how she went about accumulating it before. And Jud could make good use of it. It would make it possible for him to settle down, if that was what he wanted, or it could enable him to continue his restless wandering—henceforth in comfort and ease. She pressed the bulging pocket wistfully; it would have been wonderful to share the future with him, with or without the money.

But it hadn't worked out that way. In his need to help her, to see her name cleared, he had accomplished the opposite.

"You hear me, woman?"

Auralee turned slowly, faced Hunter. Doubling the jacket, she handed it to him. Conger had moved to the window and was looking out nervously.

"Thank you, Jud—for everything," she said,

unable to meet the hurt that was in his eyes. "It was like Jack said, at the start, but it all changed, became different later. I really meant all those things I said.

"I'm sorry it has to end this way. Back there when we crossed the border and I told you I wanted to forget Nogales, go to some other place, I was thinking of you and me, of a life together— but there's no use talking about it now. I want you to go, Jud, while there's still time."

"The hell with that!" Hunter snapped. "You didn't kill Emory—Conger did. Aim to tell Ford it was him."

"He'd not believe you, and I was a part of it anyway, just the same as if my finger was on the trigger of the gun, too."

She had known he would refuse her suggestion to leave and was looking beyond him at the circular table with its half-dozen chairs, scattered askew around it. Jack had apparently engaged in one of his poker games the previous night. It would serve her purpose.

"Too late to run now." Conger's voice came to her through the warm hush. He was still by the window, now with a gun in his hand. "I think we can hold them off until the *Federales* get here. They'll come quick when they hear shooting— and I've got some friends—"

Auralee pushed up against Hunter. As she pressed her lips to his, she took a firm hold on the butt of his pistol with one hand and placed the other on his chest.

"Good bye, Jud," she murmured, and shoved with all her strength.

He stumbled backward, collided with a chair, fell sideways into the table. It overturned as she was whirling about. She heard him shout to her as she ran to the door and jerked it open, shout again as she leveled his pistol, held in both hands, at Tom Ford. And then she was aware of nothing else as the guns of the posse rang down a curtain of darkness.

24

Cursing, kicking free of the entangling legs of the table and chairs, Hunter regained his feet. A deafening blast of gunfire rocked the house. He saw Auralee crumple in the doorway, heard Conger yell as bullets smashed through the window and knocked the gambler to the floor.

Heedless, he lunged toward the rectangle of light and dropped beside the girl. She lay face down, hair spreading over one shoulder and onto the dusty floor, arms outstretched, his pistol still clutched in her small hands.

A savage rage shook him. Snatching up the weapon, he leaped upright, hurled himself through the doorway, eyes locked to the mounted figure of Tom Ford. A gun crackled almost in his face, it seemed. The bullet struck him, spun him about, sent him sprawling onto the hard ground.

Stunned, he fought himself to a sitting position, struggled further to rise. A dim shape moved forward, wrenched the pistol from his fingers and tossed it beyond reach.

From somewhere in the layers of smoke and dust a voice said: "You want me to finish the job, Mr. Ford? Only hit in the shoulder."

The rancher's reply was low, indifferent. "No need. It's all over now. He didn't know what it was all about. Just another fool she took in."

The mist was clearing. Jud, ignoring pain, pulled himself to his feet. He was still holding the jacket Auralee had returned to him and he let it fall, needing the hand since the other hung useless at his side.

"She didn't do it!" he said, pointing at Ford. "You hear that, you goddamned sonofabitch? It wasn't her. Was him—Conger—laying in there by the window!"

The rancher, still mounted and in the center of the line of posse members, stirred slightly. "She was in on it. Had to be."

Beyond him, outside the wire fence, soldiers were pounding up. Other men were approaching, coming from nearby houses, attracted by the flurry of gunshots.

"Ought to kill you," Hunter said evenly. He was calmer now as the passing moments had their leavening effect upon him. "Maybe some-day I will."

"Done what I had to," Ford replied quietly.

"Hounding her the way you did, was like she was some kind of an animal, not a woman. I tried to make her wait, let me talk to you, tell you it was Conger that shot your brother, but she said no, you wouldn't listen. I reckon she was right. Your kind never will. You're always so god-damned right, no matter what."

Tom Ford shrugged. "Could be," he said.

Federales were crowding into the yard, rifles ready in their hands. One of the riders dismounted, stepped up to the officer in charge, said something in rapid Spanish.

The Mexican nodded, crossed to Ford, who handed him a folded sheet of paper that he took from his pocket. The officer read it briefly, glanced at Auralee and returned it. Evidently it was the rancher's authority to enter Mexico. Hunter saw the *Federales'* attention then switch to him, heard him ask a question. The interpreter, one of Ford's posse, relayed the words to Ford.

"Tell the *commandante* to let him go," the rancher said. "He come out on the short end of a string, too."

The officer listened to the rider, bobbed his head, spoke a few words of his own. The posse member turned to Jud.

"The captain says you can pull out but to get across the border *pronto.* He don't want you hanging around."

Hunter turned slowly, picked up his pistol and slid it into its holster. He retrieved the jacket, dropped after he came through the doorway, clamped it under his stiffening arm and looked down at Auralee.

She was as beautiful in death as in life. Her hair was spread about her face and shoulders in a dark, soft halo. Her skin, despite the punishment of the merciless sun, still had a fair, velvety texture. *The end of a dream,* he thought bleakly. *The finish of what might have been.*

"Aiming to bury her first," he said.

The rider shook his head. "You ain't got the time. Captain's ordering you to—"

"To hell with him!"

"You bucking for a couple of years in a Mexican jail? Take my advice, friend, move on. Mr. Ford'll have her put away decent."

Hunter's head snapped up. He touched the rancher with a hating stare. "Don't want him having anything to do with her." Then he glanced at the puncher. "Can I figure on you seeing to it?"

The man turned to Ford questioningly. The older man nodded. Jud lowered his eyes again to the girl.

"So long," he murmured, and then, walking stiff and straight, crossed to where the chestnut was waiting in the shade of a tree. Cramming the jacket into his saddlebags, he swung onto the gelding and rode from the yard.

Center Point Large Print
600 Brooks Road / PO Box 1
Thorndike, ME 04986-0001 USA

(207) 568-3717

US & Canada:
1 800 929-9108
www.centerpointlargeprint.com